Y2K-9:
The Dog Who
Saved the World

Other books by Todd Strasser

Help! I'm Trapped in My Lunch Lady's Body

Help! I'm Trapped in a Movie Star's Body

Help! I'm Trapped in My Principal's Body

Help! I'm Trapped in My Camp Counselor's Body

Help! I'm Trapped in an Alien's Body

Help! I'm Trapped in Obedience School Again

Help! I'm Trapped in Santa's Body

Help! I'm Trapped in the First Day of Summer Camp

Camp Run-a-Muck series:

#1: Greasy Grimy Gopher Guts

#2: Mutilated Monkey Meat

#3: Chopped Up Little Birdy's Feet

Help! I'm Trapped in My Sister's Body

Help! I'm Trapped in the President's Body

Help! I'm Trapped in My Gym Teacher's Body

Howl-A-Ween

Help! I'm Trapped in Obedience School

Abe Lincoln for Class President

Help! I'm Trapped in the First Day of School

Please Don't Be Mine, Julie Valentine

Help! I'm Trapped in My Teacher's Body

The Diving Bell

The Mall from Outer Space

Y2K-9

THE DOG WHO SAVED THE WORLD

TODD STRASSER

AN
APPLE
PAPERBACK

SCHOLASTIC INC.
New York Toronto London Auckland Sydney
Mexico City New Delhi Hong Kong

ISBN 0-439-14247-4

Copyright © 1999 by Todd Strasser. All rights reserved. Published by Scholastic Inc. SCHOLASTIC, APPLE PAPERBACKS, and associated logos are trademarks and/or registered trademarks of Scholastic Inc.

12 11 10 9 8 7 6 5   0 1 2 3 4/0

Printed in the U.S.A.   40

First Scholastic printing, November 1999

*To everyone at Scholastic.
Without you guys I would have
gone to the dogs.*

Y2K-9:
The Dog Who
Saved the World

MONDAY, DECEMBER 27, 1999
0200 HRS

It was two A.M. and I was in a private chat room on the Internet with my friends. On-line I went by my real name, Byte.

Byte: Merry Xmas, guys! Get good stuff?
Buffhunk: All nu weights! What'd u get?
Byte: Nu bed.
Richgurl: Wow, sounds exciting! ;-0
Byte: I'll sleep well. What'd u get, Rich?
Richgurl: BMW 5 series. Deep blue.
Foxybabe: I am soooo jealous!
Byte: How bout u, Foxy?
Foxybabe: New miniskirt. Gr8 4 dancing!
Richgurl: Ooh-la-la!
Buffhunk: Subject change: U guys ready 4
             Y2K?
Foxybabe: Ready 4 what?
Buffhunk: The government's going 2 mess up.
Richgurl: Buff's right.
Byte: Don't fly on 12/31/99.

Richgurl: I won't leave my mansion.
Buffhunk: I'm stocking up. Food, water, muscle
formulas.
Foxybabe: U're crazy. 12/31/1999 I party all
night.

Sound like your typical dull chat room conversation? Maybe, but we weren't your average group of sleepless computer geeks. We'd found one another slowly over a period of months. I'd never actually met any of them, but we'd gotten to know one another pretty well.

We may have seemed like very different kinds of people, but we all had one thing in common. Each of us had once been a high-level agent working for a secret government intelligence agency. In other words, we'd all been spies.

Foxybabe: Buff, u really hoarding food and
water?
Buffhunk: Definitely.
Richgurl: Toilet paper, 2.
Byte: Never thought of that!
Richgurl: Have to think what u'll really need.
Buffhunk: Government's run by losers. Be
prepared!

If we sounded bitter it was because we had something else in common, too. Not only were we former spies, but we had all been "put out to pasture." That means when the agencies we'd worked for no longer had any use for us, they'd thrown us out.

> Foxybabe: U should have more f8th in our government.
> Buffhunk: Y? They never had f8th in me. I wanted 2 spend my life with CIA. But they dumped me like an old shoe.
> Byte: Hate 2 say it, but I agree with Buff. U risk ur life 4 ur country. But when they don't need u anymore, it's bye-bye.

Suddenly an Instant Message box popped up on my screen.

URGENT!
Byte—Go to AIA-SCR3 immediately.
I'll meet you there.
—Lassie

Lassie? I stared at the screen in disbelief. What in the world could *she* want?

I signed off from the chat room but didn't go to SCR3 right away. I had to think first. SCR3 was short for Secret Chat Room 3. It was a secure locale run by the AIA for its operatives. In other words, it was a chat room for spies.

Until two years before, I'd been a high-level AIA spy. I'd put my life on the line for my country. I'd risked injury and death. I'd faced dangers no human would be expected to face. And then I'd been retired. As far as the AIA was concerned, I was finished.

Lassie had been my case officer at the AIA, my boss. It was she who put me out to pasture.

As I sat in that dark room and stared at the computer screen, I knew there was no reason that I had to answer Lassie's Instant Message. The AIA had used me and then thrown me away like a chewed-over bone. I owed them nothing.

And yet a sense of duty to my country still

4

haunted me. Lassie had always been good to me. When she put me out to pasture we both knew she was only following orders.

I sighed and gave in. The least I could do was see what she wanted.

Lassie was waiting for me when I arrived.

Lassie: U there, Byte?
Byte: Am now.
Lassie: Been a long time. Have a nice Xmas?
Byte: Cut 2 the chase, Lass.
Lassie: U're still bitter about what happened?
Byte: Wouldn't u be?
Lassie: Yes.
Byte: Wazup?
Lassie: I need u.
Byte: What 4?
Lassie: Can't say here. Need F2F.

She was asking for a face-to-face meeting.

Byte: Not easy, Lass. I have a family now. Responsibilities.
Lassie: It's urgent, Byte. Code Z.

Once again, I stared at the screen in amazement. Code Z was the highest level of danger. It went beyond mere life and death. It meant our entire nation was facing the threat of destruction.

Byte: Serious?
Lassie: Think I'd bother u otherwise?
Byte: U're right.
Lassie: Today at 1230 hrs. The old place.
Byte: I'll think about it.
Lassie: Think hard, Byte. Ur country needs u.

And just like that, she was gone. I sat at the computer for a long time without moving. Should I meet with Lassie or not? I yawned and decided to sleep on it.

MONDAY, DECEMBER 27, 1999
0800 HRS

I was in my new bed when I heard a door creak upstairs. Then footsteps coming down. From the sound of those footsteps I knew it was Benjy Barkley, age eight, the youngest member of the Barkley family.

I stretched and yawned as Benjy entered the kitchen. He was a thin, wiry boy with short brown hair and shoelaces that were never tied. Of all the members of the Barkley family, I liked him the most. Probably because he was the only one who paid any attention to me.

Benjy bent down and rubbed my head. "Hi, Byte, how'd you sleep?"

With one eye open, I thought.

But Benjy had already gone over to the refrigerator and pulled open the door. The kid was eighty pounds of nonstop energy. I had to smile. He kind of reminded me of myself as a pup.

Benjy's parents, Barb and Brad Barkley, were the next to enter the kitchen. Mr. Barkley was an average-size man with brown hair and a bit of a gut. He was wearing his business clothes. He was a police detective.

Mrs. Barkley was an inch taller than her husband and a lot thinner. She was wearing a red-and-black jogging outfit.

I noticed that Mr. Barkley was carrying a phone bill.

"I just don't get it, Barb," he said. "Three or four hours of phone charges every single night. And yet I know we're all asleep."

"What does the phone company say?" Mrs. Barkley asked as she poured both of them cups of coffee.

"They say someone in this house is definitely using the phone," answered Mr. Barkley. "They just can't figure out who."

"Well, it's not you and it's not me," said Mrs. Barkley. "And Benjy's in bed and asleep most nights by eight. So who does that leave?"

Mr. Barkley sighed. "All right, I'll talk to her."

The last set of footsteps down the stairs belonged to Brandy, the Barkleys' twelve-year-old daughter. She was long and thin like her mother and liked khakis, turtleneck sweaters, and boys. She also had a major set of braces.

"Brandy, have you been going on-line late at night?" Mr. Barkley asked.

"Oh, no, not this again," Brandy groaned. "How many times do I have to tell you the answer is no?"

"Then how do you explain these calls?" Mr. Barkley showed her the phone bill.

"I've told you a hundred times, don't ask me," Brandy snapped. She pointed at Benjy, who was sitting at the kitchen table eating a bowl of cereal. "Ask Mr. Action Figure over there."

"You're whacked, metal mouth," Benjy snorted. "I sleep at night."

"I know he does, Brandy," said Mr. Barkley. "It has to be you."

"It's not!" Brandy insisted. "Do I look like someone who's been up all night?"

Mr. Barkley shook his head wearily. "I just don't understand it."

"Maybe it's the dog," Brandy joked.

"You leave Byte out of this, tinsel teeth!" Benjy yelled. He jumped up and brought his cereal bowl over to the kitchen sink. "Did anyone give Byte breakfast?"

The rest of the Barkleys glanced at one another. No one answered.

"Why do I even bother to ask?" Benjy grumbled. "Does anyone in this family even care about this dog besides me?"

"We all do," answered Mrs. Barkley.

"Then how come I'm the only one who ever re-

9

members to feed him?" Benjy asked as he scooped dog food into my bowl.

It was a good question and I was glad Benjy had asked it. As soon as the scoop left the bowl, my face went in.

Life with the Barkleys wasn't very exciting. But it was comfortable. I was fed each morning and evening (as long as Benjy remembered) and got to sleep in my nice new bed. Benjy and I had fun playing fetch with the Frisbee and going for walks.

In return I performed my job, which was to bark fiercely whenever a stranger came to the front door. Basically, I was a guard dog. Other dogs in the neighborhood were proud to have that job. They thought it made them more important than those little yappy lap dogs who ran away yelping at the slightest scent of danger.

But I'd once been a spy. A bomb-sniffing demolition expert with a genetically enhanced nose capable of smelling things no normal dog would notice. To me, being a guard dog was like going from the star quarterback on the football team to the water boy.

Maybe that was part of the reason I was

11

tempted to meet with Lassie. That and the fact that except for Benjy, everyone around the Barkley household took me for granted. Life was good, but I needed some excitement.

After breakfast Mr. Barkley went to work. Since it was the week between Christmas and New Year's, the kids headed off to play with their friends. Mrs. Barkley worked out of the house, so she went upstairs to her office.

I had time to kill, so I took a nap. Around noon I looked up at the kitchen clock. Was I sure I wanted to see Lassie? Did I really want to get involved with the AIA again after what they'd done to me?

I scratched my half-ear with my back paw. (I'd lost the other half in a nasty fight with a Russian wolfhound.) A nagging sense of curiosity tugged at me like a leash. Oh, heck, I decided, I'd go see what she wanted.

I went through the back door and out to the yard, then dragged the garden hose over to the flower bed. Since it was the middle of winter, the bed was just dirt. But it was a warm, sunny day and the dirt was loose.

I found a strong stick and wedged it into the garden faucet. Then I pushed the stick with my head until the faucet turned and water started to run through the hose.

Back at the flower bed I let the water run for

twenty minutes. Finally I turned off the faucet and dragged the hose away. The flower bed was a sea of soupy brown mud. I had to smile to myself. This was going to be fun.

Woof! Woof! A little while later I stood outside the back door and barked. In the reflection of the window I could see that I'd gone from a sleek yellow Labrador retriever to a lumpy chocolate one.

I kept barking until Mrs. Barkley came down to see what the matter was.

"Oh, my gosh, Byte!" she cried when she saw me. "What in the world did you get into? You're covered from head to foot. All right, don't go anywhere. I'll get the car and we'll clean you up."

Mrs. Barkley disappeared back into the house. I went over to the backyard gate and waited for her to bring the car around. I couldn't help smiling to myself as I recalled how proud the Barkleys had been the day they "taught" me to roll over. If only they knew how easy it was for me to "teach" them to drive me places.

Mrs. Barkley took me straight to Groomingdale's, the local pet salon.

"My, my, my," said the salon's owner, Ms. Shepherd, when Mrs. Barkley walked me in. "Looks like we've had a lot of fun playing in the mud. But now we'll have to pay for it, won't we?"

Ms. Shepherd bared her teeth in a nasty smile. "Shall we clip his nails and give him an ear treatment, too?"

"Oh, all right," Mrs. Barkley answered. "Is Trixie here?"

Trixie was the lady who usually did the dirty work.

"She called in sick today," said Ms. Shepherd. "But I have a nice young Irishwoman filling in for her."

Lassie came out from the back. She was wearing a white smock. Her bright red hair was pulled back in a ponytail. She gave me a wink. I noticed that she'd changed the style of her glasses. It had been a long time since we'd seen each other.

"Give that mongrel the works," Ms. Shepherd growled as soon as Mrs. Barkley left.

"Right away, ma'am," Lassie replied, and led me into the back.

Boy, I couldn't help thinking, *if only Ms. Shepherd knew who she was bossing around!*

In the back Lassie closed the doors. Now it was just she and I and a couple of yammering puffball poodles who seemed to spend more time in the salon than they did at home. Lassie helped me into a steel tub and gently sprayed me with warm water to rinse off the mud.

"Well, Byte, it's good to see you again," she said. "It's been a dog's age."

I rolled my eyes.

"You made the right decision, Byte," she said. "I'm proud of you. If you can help us, your country will be proud of you, too."

I gave myself a hard shake and made sure I got her good and wet.

"Still angry, I see." Lassie wiped muddy drops of water off her glasses. "I was hoping that maybe after all this time you'd mellowed a little. Are the Barkleys being good to you?"

I shrugged.

"They seem like a nice family," Lassie said. "They don't suspect anything, do they?"

I shook my head. As far as the Barkleys were concerned, I was your basic sleepy watchdog.

"Do they feed you well?" Lassie asked.

I wasn't the type of dog who enjoyed small talk. I let out an impatient sigh and planted myself squarely over my paws as if preparing to give her another good spraying.

"I get the message, Byte," Lassie said. "Okay, here's the story. As you know, Y2K is almost here. The NSA, the CIA, and the FBI have been flooded with threats from terrorist groups claiming they're going to strike at the stroke of midnight on December 31, 1999. In case you've

16

forgotten, that's four days from now."

The CIA was the Central Intelligence Agency. The FBI was the Federal Bureau of Investigation. And the NSA, or National Security Agency, was the ultimate spy agency. More secretive and powerful than both the FBI and the CIA.

I gave her a "so what else is new?" look.

"Yes, I know," Lassie said as she started to lather me up. "There have been hundreds of threats about Y2K, and most of them have turned out to be nothing. But the threats keep coming. The problem is that with all the budget cutbacks and people away on vacation at this time of year, we don't have the manpower to track each one of them down."

I rolled my eyes impatiently. That turned out to be really dumb because I got soap in them and it stung. Why was she telling me this? I wasn't a government agent anymore.

"As you know, Byte," Lassie said, and went on lathering my fur, "for several years now the country has been preparing for the Y2K bug. We've gone over all the possible computer networks that might fail. What most people don't know is that we've also been trying to safeguard those networks against a terrorist attack. The banking system, the air traffic control system, the electric power grids, the highway system — every possible computer network has been checked out."

I remembered now that Lassie always took her

17

time making a point. The problem was, I *hated* baths! If she wanted to take her time filling me in on the details, why couldn't we do it over a bowl of dog biscuits?

"Every government agency responsible for national security—the FBI, the CIA, the NSA—has been making sure the major computer systems are safeguarded against terrorist acts," Lassie went on. "Not every rumor can be taken seriously, but I am very worried about one threat in particular. My superiors don't think it's serious, but I do."

I raised an eyebrow skeptically. Was she saying what I thought she was saying?

"Yes, Byte," Lassie said. "By coming to you, I'm disobeying orders. That's how strongly I feel about this threat."

I was beginning to understand why Lassie wanted to see me. I just wished she'd start rinsing me off already!

"I'll be honest," Lassie went on. "Some of the people in the AIA think the mission I want you for is silly. Some of my coworkers have even laughed at me for taking it seriously. But I think they're being unfairly dogmatic."

I let out another big sigh. It figured. The mission she wanted me for was the one everyone else thought was a joke.

"I think they're wrong," Lassie said. "I think this is a huge and very dangerous threat. And that's why I've come to you, Byte. Next, you probably want to know why you should help me."

I nodded.

Lassie cupped her hands in front of her. "Byte, I need you. The *whole country* needs you. Believe me, after what the AIA did to you, you were the last dog I wanted to approach. I mean, forcing you into retirement was a disgrace."

Arf! It sure was! And to think that I was only *six* when they did it! *Six years old!* A dog in his prime! It was a painful memory. I had to blink back the tears. Darn that soap!

"You know I fought as hard as I could for you," Lassie said. "But the AIA has its rules. You were over forty in dog years. That's the age when we're required to take you out of the field. And don't forget, we did offer you a desk job."

Ha! The thought of it! Me, ex-spy and explosives expert, sitting in the typing pool with those gossiping poodles! I might not have been a lion, but I still had my pride!

"Don't make me beg, Byte," Lassie said. "Throw me a bone here. We both know you're unique. No one else can do what you can do. We need your special talent desperately."

I didn't react. Now it was Lassie's turn to sigh.

"I see that you've only been listening with half an ear," she said. "I wish I knew how to make you understand the seriousness of this situation. If this terrorist threat is real . . . if these terrorists

19

actually have found a weakness that we don't know about . . . if they truly can bring the country to a halt, it could be the end of civilization as we know it. Think about it, Byte. No more warm doggy bed. No more regular meals. On January 1, 2000, you could be out in the woods, fighting over food scraps with other animals and sleeping on the cold ground. We all could."

Did she think she could scare me?

"I'm not trying to scare you, Byte," Lassie said as if she could read my mind. "I just want you to understand how serious this is. So what do you think, Byte, will you help me? Can I count on you?"

I didn't know the answer yet. All I knew was that I was tired of standing in that dumb metal tub filled with warm water. And I was tired of being covered with suds.

I gave myself another hard shake. White soapsuds flew everywhere.

"Gee, thanks, Byte!" Lassie stepped back and wiped her glasses on the hem of her white smock. Then she picked up the sprayer. "Sorry, I didn't mean to lose my temper. Let me rinse you off."

Lassie rinsed off the suds and then used the blow-dryer to dry me. It felt good to be pampered.

"You want your nails clipped?" she asked.

I can't say that I liked having my nails clipped. But I was enjoying the attention.

Lassie got out the nail clipper and went to work. When she was finished, she picked up a nail file and smoothed off the rough edges. Now *that* was what I called service!

Finally, Lassie picked up a mirror and slowly walked around me so that I could see the finished product. There I was, washed, brushed, clipped, and polished. I have to tell you, I was one fine-lookin' pooch!

Lassie lowered the mirror and gave me a serious look. "Will you do it, Byte? It would mean a lot to me."

She batted her eyes and gave me a needy look. It was the old damsel-in-distress routine. She was stuck in a snowbank and I was her Saint Bernard. She was surrounded by bad guys and I was her Rin Tin Tin. A bear was approaching and I was her big red dog, Clifford.

How could I say no?

Arf! I nodded.

"Oh, thank you, Byte!" Lassie threw her arms around my neck and gave me a hug. "I can't begin to tell you how important this could be to our country. Now I'm going to show you something. It's the only link we have to this terrorist group."

Lassie opened a manila envelope and took out a single sheet of wrinkled white paper. A message written with cutout letters said the following:

Attention United States. Prepare to meet your end. At midnight December 31, 1999, this country

WILL GO DOWN the DRAIN UN-
LESS the FOLLOWING demands
are met:
  1. We want One billion
     dollars in Cash by noon
     On December 31.
  2. We want an Official
     Letter hand-signed by the
     President Of the United
     States giving us the right
     to alter the LINCOLN
     Memorial in any way
     We Choose.
THIS is no joke.   PHLUSH

I felt a frown come over my face. The first demand was typical. All terrorist organizations
needed money. But the second demand was
downright weird.

"We have no idea who PHLUSH is," Lassie
said. "We assume it's an acronym, but we don't
know what it stands for. Needless to say, the second demand is a mystery."

I nodded.

"I was able to get a friend of mine in the NSA,

a top fingerprint guy, to check out the letter," Lassie went on. "He came up with a print, but we've found no matches among known terrorists. Another friend of mine is trying to track down the magazines the letters came from."

Basically, she was saying that she had no real leads.

"As you can imagine, this has to be top secret," Lassie said. "If my superiors at the AIA or the NSA find out I've disobeyed orders and come to you, I'll be in the doghouse. So I have to ask you a favor. I want you to work alone."

Ruff! I shook my head. Lassie frowned.

"I just explained why, Byte," she said. "If anyone finds out, it could cost me my job."

Arf! I nodded.

"You know that and yet you want to work with someone," Lassie said. "Someone outside the intelligence community?"

Arf! I nodded.

"And you're *sure* they can be trusted?" Lassie asked.

I gave her a look.

"You're right," Lassie said. "I guess it doesn't matter at this point. Okay, I have no choice but to trust you on this. I'll arrange for you to have a secure apartment for a base of operations. I'll supply you with a car, surveillance equipment, and cash. Now, Byte, are you ready?"

Arf!

Lassie held the terrorist's letter in front of my nose. I took a long, hard sniff. The note hardly smelled of anything more than printer's ink. But deep in my genetically engineered brain, I'd locked onto a scent that even my nose wasn't aware of. I would know the next time I smelled it.

"Got it?" Lassie asked.

Arf!

"Great. Now, is there anything else you think you'll need?"

Arf! I nodded.

Lassie frowned. "What?"

I cocked my head and gave her a disappointed look. How soon they forget.

"Oh, of course!" Lassie slapped her forehead. "An unlimited supply of rawhide bones."

Arf! I smiled and nodded. *Now we were talking!*

MONDAY, DECEMBER 27, 1999
2330 HRS

That night I waited until the Barkleys went to sleep, then got on the computer and went into the chat room. My friends were already there.

Buffhunk: Benched 335 2day! I am cut!
Foxybabe: U must be a hunk! Send me a pic?
Buffhunk: Can't, Foxy. Scanner's down.
Richgurl: Been down long time, Buff.
Byte: Lo, everyone.
Buffhunk: Byte, what happened 2 u last night?
Foxybabe: U disappeared.
Byte: Something came up.
Richgurl: She cute? ;-)
Byte: Yes.
Buffhunk: Way 2 go!
Byte: Not like that.
Foxybabe: Sure, Byte.
Byte: Serious news, guys. Ur country needs u.
Richgurl: Yeah, right. LOL!
Byte: Code Z.

Foxybabe: O-O. U're losing Ur grip, Byte.
Byte: Want 2 hear?
Buffhunk: Y not? Nothing better 2 do.
Richgurl: Me 2.
Byte: Here's the story.

I told them everything Lassie had told me. How the NSA, the FBI, and the CIA were overwhelmed with Y2K matters. How Lassie had come to me because she believed an unknown group of terrorists was planning to bring down the United States on New Year's Eve 1999.

Foxybabe: This is hard 2 swallow, Byte.
Richgurl: I agree.
Buffhunk: U seem like nice guy, Byte. But u
          have 2 admit it's wild story. Why
          should u believe Lassie?
Byte: I know her. If she's willing to risk her job,
      she must have good reason.
Richgurl: Can u prove any of this is true?
Byte: Tomorrow morning u'll each receive
      plane tix + $300 expense money + further instructions.
Richgurl: It's starting 2 sound real.
Buffhunk: Yeah, I have feeling I'll be seeing u
          guys soon.

I waited in bed for the Barkleys to come down for breakfast. As usual, Benjy was the first to arrive.

"Hey, Byte, want some breakfast?" he asked as he bent down and rubbed my head.

I pushed myself up to my feet. I sure did want some breakfast. It was going to be a long day, and I had no way of knowing when I might eat again.

I was having my dog food when Mr. and Mrs. Barkley came into the kitchen, followed a moment later by Brandy.

"It's just driving me crazy, Barb," Mr. Barkley was saying to his wife. "Night after night, three or four hours of telephone time on the computer line. It doesn't make sense."

"I know what's happening!" Benjy suddenly said.

I jerked my head up from my food bowl. Had I been caught?

"You know how people talk in their sleep and

sleepwalk?" Benjy asked. "Maybe one of us is sleep-computing."

"What a moron!" Brandy groaned.

"That's enough, Brandy," Mrs. Barkley snapped. "That's no way to talk about your brother."

"Give me a break, Mom," Brandy shot back. "Sleep-computing? The next thing you know, he'll be talking about sleep-eating."

"Funny you should mention that." Mr. Barkley patted his big belly. "The other night I found myself in my pajamas staring into the refrigerator. I have no idea how I got there."

"Have stomach, will travel," Mrs. Barkley quipped.

"I'm just saying, maybe there's something to Benjy's theory," Mr. Barkley said.

"You're all so weird." Brandy rolled her eyes. "Why not blame it on aliens who sneak into our house every night and use the computer? Or Santa Claus. Better yet, maybe it really is Byte."

The Barkleys all turned and looked at me. It was time to go into my "dumb dog" act. I sat up, opened my mouth, and let my tongue hang out. Then I panted happily and wagged my tail.

"Isn't he cute?" Benjy grinned. "He knows we're talking about him."

"Could you imagine him on the computer?" Mr. Barkley chuckled.

"E-barking with his dog friends," said Mrs. Barkley.

"Playing cool dog video games," said Benjy.

"Downloading pictures of dog babes," said Mr. Barkley.

"Brad!" Mrs. Barkley gasped. "Not in front of the children!"

Mr. Barkley's face turned red. "Just joking, kids."

"You guys are totally mental," muttered Brandy.

"Lighten up," Mr. Barkley said. "We're having some fun."

"Talk about fun," said Mrs. Barkley, "what are you kids planning for New Year's Eve?"

The conversation veered off into what everyone wanted to do for the biggest New Year's Eve celebration in 1,000 years. I decided to go into the living room and lie down on the rug for a quick nap. But as I left the kitchen, I couldn't help looking back over my shoulder at the Barkleys. I was surprised to discover that I felt kind of bad about leaving them. Especially Benjy. I just hoped he'd understand someday.

I waited until Mr. Barkley went to work and the kids left to hang out with their friends. Then I took off. Being an unleashed dog in the city always involves some element of risk. There are police, the ASPCA, animal shelter workers, and everyday good Samaritans who want to bring you back home.

But part of my AIA training had involved evasive tactics to avoid those situations. As I made my way toward the capital, running through yards and back alleys, I just hoped the rest of my friends were also on their way.

It wasn't long before I passed the Washington Monument and the Lincoln Memorial and entered a park. A little while later I arrived at a big plaque that read:

William Jefferson Clinton Dog Run
"Where dogs still run free!"

31

The dog run was a large fenced-off area of lawn. It was a warm, sunny day, unusual for late December. The run was filled with dogs. Outside the fence their masters watched and chatted. I slipped in through the gate and pretended to mix with my fellow canines.

Now it was time to find my friends. Due to the top secret nature of our mission, I had decided not to have them wear any telltale objects of identification. No red flowers in their lapels. No carefully placed yellow bandannas around their necks.

Instead, I felt confident that I would be able to recognize them. Over the many months that we'd shared our private chat room, I'd gotten a mental picture of each of them.

Richgurl lived in a mansion and had tons of money. I guessed she was middle-aged and would be wearing lots of jewels. Buffhunk spent hours each day pumping iron. No doubt those muscles would bulge through his clothes. Foxybabe was the type who loved to go out dancing all night. I figured she'd be the youngest of the group. And probably a blond.

I cruised along the fence, studying the faces of the humans who stood outside. I assumed that my friends wouldn't be hard to spot for another reason—they wouldn't be carrying leashes.

But as I trotted along I saw that a lot of people weren't carrying leashes. It was such a nice day that even folks who didn't own dogs were stopping to look.

I continued along the edge of the fence, looking up at the humans who lined it. Which ones were my friends? Was Richgurl the gorgeous woman with the wavy black hair? Was Buffhunk the broad-shouldered guy with the piercing blue eyes? Suddenly I realized that finding them might be harder than I thought.

I kept circling the inside of the fence, waiting and watching. Gradually, the faces began to change as people took their dogs and left and new dog owners arrived. The people without dogs came and went, too. But one face didn't change. And instead of watching the dogs, she kept looking around at the other people. Just what I would have expected.

The trouble was, she didn't come close to fitting the image of any of my friends. She couldn't have been older than fourteen, much too young to have worked for the government. Especially in one of the top intelligence agencies. Not only that, but her hair was spiky and dyed purple. Her ears were filled with hoops, and her nose and eyebrow were pierced. Strangest of all, she was wearing a black leather dog collar with silver studs!

Talk about bad taste!

I assumed that she was waiting for a friend or boyfriend.

I moved on, but for some reason my nose kept

bringing me back to her. It was as if there were something about her scent, something that *smelled* like a spy.

It just didn't make sense. Intelligence agencies liked to employ different sorts of people. The ones you wouldn't expect to be spies were always the best. But there were laws against using minors in such dangerous professions.

I kept circling the fence, looking for someone else.

But something kept leading me back to her. If I forgot what she was supposed to look like, if I didn't think about her age, then she did fit the description of the person I was searching for. She had no dog. She was looking around for someone. She looked like the sort of person who liked to party.

Could she possibly be Foxybabe?

Time was passing. If I didn't make contact with my friends soon, they might get tired of waiting and leave. Finally, I decided to take a chance. I went over to the girl with the purple hair, put my paws against the fence, and stood on my hind legs facing her.

She instantly frowned. "Go away! Shoo!"

That was a good sign. She definitely wasn't there because she liked dogs.

Now what? I wondered. I had an idea. The ground inside the dog run was bare and loose. I started to drag my paw through it. By the time I finished the letter *B*, the girl with the purple hair was staring at me.

I did the *Y* next and looked up at her. Her eyebrows were tilted down.

The *T* was easy. I looked up at her and barked. She stared at me and then at the letters I'd carved in the ground.

"Is this a joke?" she asked.

Ruff! I shook my head.

She blinked in disbelief. "You understand me?"

Arf! I nodded.

"No way," she said, mostly to herself. "I don't believe this. Okay, dog, roll over. . . . No, wait! That's too easy. Hop on your back feet, walk backward, and bark four times."

I rose up on my hind legs and staggered backward. *Woof! Woof! Woof! Woof!*

The girl with the purple hair put her hand on her forehead and looked pale. "I don't believe this! I really don't believe this! I came all this way to meet *a dog*?"

A man standing at the fence a dozen feet away turned and scowled. I lifted my paw and pressed it against my snout.

"Oh, no! Now he's telling me to be quiet!" she gasped. "I really must be losing it!"

I backed away and watched the others around us nervously. Several people were staring. This was not good. A former agent would know better than to make a scene. Did she want to blow my cover? Or had I just made a huge mistake?

It was time to take evasive action. I headed for the gate.

"Hey! Wait!" she cried and started around the fence.

I went through the gate when a lady opened it for her pug. The girl with the purple hair was waiting for me.

"What is this?" she asked loudly as I trotted past. I looked over my shoulder at her. Before we could communicate, I had to get as far away from the crowd as possible. Otherwise, she was going to attract attention with that loud voice.

I headed for some woods. I kept glancing over my shoulder to make sure she was still following me. Finally I stopped when I thought I was far enough away so that the others wouldn't hear.

"You're a dog," she said.

Arf! I nodded. *Duh!*

"You understand everything I say?"

Arf!

"Amazing!"

I tapped my paw impatiently. I already knew *my* story. What was hers? Who was she?

"You're Byte?" she asked.

Arf! Again I nodded. At this rate I was going to get a major cramp in my neck.

"This has to be the weirdest thing I've ever seen," she said.

Oh, really? I thought. *I'm not the one wearing the studded dog collar!*

Woof! I barked impatiently. She still hadn't told me who she was.

"Huh? What are you barking at me for?" she asked.

Grrrrr. I snarled just a little.

She took a step back as if she were scared. "Oh, I get it. You want to know who I am?"

Arf! I nodded in relief. *Yahoo!*

"Well, I don't know how you figured it out," she said. "But I'm Richgurl."

I tilted my head and gave her a puzzled look.

Richgurl put her hands on her hips. "What? You don't think I look rich? I lied, okay? And look who's talking, I mean, barking. You lied about who you were, too."

Grrrrrrr. Ruff! I barked angrily and shook my head.

Richgurl took another step back. "Hey, chill! Okay, maybe you're right. You didn't lie about who you were. But you didn't exactly come out and say you were a dog, either."

I shrugged.

"Listen, pooch," Richgurl said. "Everybody on the Internet lies. You really think Buffhunk and Foxybabe are what they say they are? Give me a break. Why do you think we always came up with those lame excuses for not sending one another our pictures?"

I'd never thought of that. Suddenly I felt my fur go up. What if she was right? I looked back toward the dog run. Were Buffhunk and Foxybabe still there? Had they given up and left?

"You want to find the others, right?" Richgurl guessed.

Arf! I took a step back toward the run, but Richgurl hadn't moved. I gave her a puzzled look.

"Sorry, Byte," she groaned. "I still can't believe I'm talking to a dog."

Woof! I barked impatiently.

"Okay, okay, keep your fur on!" Richgurl started to follow.

TUESDAY, DECEMBER 28, 1999
1250 HRS

Back at the dog run fence, Richgurl nodded across the way at a heavyset bald guy with a bushy beard.

"Guess who that is?" she asked.

Woof? I couldn't imagine.

"He got here about the same time I did, and he's been looking around ever since," Richgurl said. "No leash, either. I can just about promise you that's Buffhunk."

No way! It couldn't be. Buffhunk spent hours each day in a gym. He had muscles growing on muscles. He only ate bean sprouts grown in vitamins and steroids. The guy across the way was shaped like a grown-up Teletubby and looked like he'd spent most of his life in a McDonald's washing down multiple Quarter Pounders and french fries with super-sized chocolate thick shakes.

Richgurl started around the fence toward him. "Come on, Byte, this'll be fun."

We went up to the heavy guy. Richgurl leaned

40

against the fence next to him. I stopped next to her.

"Hi," Richgurl said with a smile.

"Uh, hi," the heavy guy replied with a scowl.

"Waiting for someone?" Richgurl asked.

"Maybe," he answered cautiously.

"Maybe someone named Byte?" Richgurl asked.

The heavyset guy frowned at her, then glanced around nervously. "Did he send you?"

"No," said Richgurl. "I came here to meet him, too."

"So where is he?" asked the heavy guy.

"He's standing right next to me," Richgurl said.

The heavyset guy looked past her. "What are you talking about? There's no one standing next to you."

"Look again," Richgurl said.

The heavyset guy looked again. "Yeah, so? There's still no one."

"You don't see a dog?" Richgurl asked.

"Yeah, I see a dog. So what?" the heavyset guy said.

"Well, let's face it, Buffhunk," Richgurl said, "you're not exactly what you pretended to be online."

"Huh?"

"Neither is Byte," Richgurl said.

The lines in Buffhunk's broad forehead deepened. He looked down at me and then back at

Richgurl. "Are you trying to tell me that Byte is a dog?"

"What if I was?" Richgurl asked.

"I'd say you'd gone mental," Buffhunk said.

Richgurl looked down at me. "What do you think, Byte?"

I cocked my head and shrugged. As far as I was concerned, Buffhunk had every right to think she was mental.

"Tell the dog to do something," Richgurl suggested to Buffhunk.

"Why?" Buffhunk asked.

"Just do it," Richgurl said.

"Sit," Buffhunk said to me.

"No, no, tell him to do something hard," Richgurl said.

"Sure." Buffhunk grinned. "Hey, dog, what's the square root of twenty-five?"

Woof! Woof! Woof! Woof! Woof! I barked five times.

Buffhunk turned pale. "How'd he do that?"

"Probably dumb luck," Richgurl answered with a sly grin. "Try another question."

"Okay," said Buffhunk. "If a rooster is sitting on a roof and it lays an egg, which side of the roof will the egg roll down?"

Grrrrrrr! I snarled and shook my head. It was a trick question! Roosters don't lay eggs.

Buffhunk's eyes bugged out. He yanked a blue bandanna out of his back pocket and dabbed some sweat off his forehead. "I'm not believing this! I came all the way here to do a secret mission *with a dog?*"

"Join the crowd," Richgurl said.

"Who are you anyway?" Buffhunk asked. "Foxybabe?"

"Nope, I'm Richgurl."

Buffhunk frowned. "You're rich?"

"You're buff?" Richgurl shot back.

"Okay, okay, I get the point," Buffhunk muttered. "But if you're Richgurl and he's Byte, then where's Foxybabe?"

That was a good question.

T he three of us gazed around the dog run. The only people who looked young enough to stay out all night partying had dogs or were holding leashes while their dogs ran around inside.

In fact, the only person standing by the fence who wasn't holding a leash was a wrinkled little old lady with white hair. The weird thing was that she wasn't dressed like a little old lady. She was wearing a white turtleneck sweater, a tight, short black miniskirt, and knee-high shiny white boots.

Oh, no! I thought.

Richgurl looked down at me. "You thinking what I'm thinking, Byte?"

I let out a small dismayed yelp.

"No way!" said Buffhunk. "You really think that old bag's Foxybabe?"

"Hey, if you can be Buffhunk, she can be Foxybabe," Richgurl answered.

"Don't get so smart," Buffhunk shot back. "You lied, too. And not just about being rich. You're way too young to have ever been a government agent."

Ruff! I barked. This wasn't the time for arguments. They could talk about being a bunch of phonies later. Richgurl and Buffhunk gave each other a look as if they were agreeing to a temporary truce.

Just then the little old white-haired lady with the high white boots left the fence. If she was Foxybabe, we'd have to hurry!

Buffhunk, Richgurl, and I rushed after her. Being a fleet-footed four-legged type, I was the fastest. Richgurl was almost able to keep up. Buffhunk lumbered behind, wheezing and gasping for air.

I reached the little old lady first and planted myself in front of her.

Woof! I barked.

The little old lady stopped and frowned at me. A moment later Richgurl jogged up.

"Excuse me, but do you go by the screen name Foxybabe?" she asked as she caught her breath.

"Who wants to know?" the little old lady asked warily, and patted her white hair with her hand.

"We do," Richgurl answered. "Because if that's your screen name, you're part of our team."

Arf! I barked.

The little old lady looked at Richgurl and me and took a step backward. "What is this? A joke?"

That's when Richgurl made a mistake. "No," she said, and stepped too close.

"*Pee Soop!*" the little old lady cried. She kicked out with one white boot and her bony hand sliced through the air in a classic Jackie Chan karate chop.

Richgurl barely managed to duck out of the way. Meanwhile the little old lady landed with one leg ready to kick again and both hands raised to fight.

"Jeez, what's with you?" Richgurl cried, and backed away.

"I know tai chi, cheep-tea, and Bruce Lee," the little old lady warned.

Now Buffhunk arrived. His face was red from running. He put his hands on his knees and bent over to catch his breath. "Sorry, guys. I didn't mean to dog it. Guess I'm out of shape."

"We're just trying to find out if you're from our chat room," Richgurl explained to the little old karate lady.

48

"I was supposed to meet three people from a chat room," answered the little old lady. "But you don't fit the description. And neither does he." She pointed at Buffhunk, then at me. "And he's a dog!"

"Yeah, well, I have news for you," said Richgurl. "That dog's Byte. And I'm Richgurl and Mr. Tubby Wubby over here is Buffhunk. And I'm willing to bet every penny I have that you're Foxybabe."

The little old lady stared at each of us with wide, astonished eyes. "Why, never in my wildest dreams!"

"Join the crowd," Buffhunk wheezed.

The little old lady nodded. "Okay, I'm Foxybabe. But you three don't look anything like you said you did."

"Look who's talking," Buffhunk scoffed. "We're supposed to believe that you're out every night partying?"

"In the old age home," Richgurl cracked.

Slap! She and Buffhunk shared a high five.

"Why, you — " Foxybabe raised her bony hands to fight again.

Grrrrrrr! Ruff! I barked angrily and jumped between them.

"Byte's right," said Buffhunk. "Maybe we're not who we said we were. But we're still a team. It's not going to work if we pick on one another."

Arf! I barked in agreement.

"Should we tell one another our real names?" Richgurl suggested.

Ruff! I shook my head.

"Why not?" asked Foxybabe.

"I bet it's a security thing," Buffhunk guessed. "The less we know about one another, the less we can reveal if we're captured."

"Captured?" Foxybabe repeated, puzzled.

"I hate to say this, Buff, but I think you've been playing too many video games," Richgurl said with a smirk.

Woof! I barked to get their attention, then started to trot away.

"Where's he going?" Richgurl asked.

"I don't know, but he's the top dog so I guess we'll follow," Buffhunk said.

"Well, I'll be doggone! Not in a million years would I have believed this," Foxybabe said as she followed, too.

Now that the team was assembled, I led the way to the car drop. Just as Lassie had promised, an unmarked Jeep was waiting in an otherwise empty parking lot. I went to the rear left tire and ran my paw over it.

Clink! The keys fell to the ground.

"Unbelievable!" Buffhunk muttered.

With my nose, I pushed the keys toward the members of my team. *Woof!* I barked. Which one of them wanted to drive?

The three of them looked at one another.

"Hey, don't look at me," said Richgurl. "I'm not old enough to drive."

"And I hate to say this," said Buffhunk, "but I never learned."

We all turned and looked at Foxybabe.

"Oh, dear," she said, patting her white hair nervously. "You don't really want me to drive, do you?"

Foxybabe hadn't driven a car in years.

"The home usually provides us with transportation," she explained as she gripped the steering wheel tightly and leaned so far forward that her chin almost bumped into her hands. Buffhunk sat in the front seat with a map on his lap. Richgurl and I were in the back.

Beep! Beep! Beep! The cars behind us kept honking their horns.

"Why are they being so rude?" Foxybabe glared into the rearview mirror.

"This is just a guess," Richgurl answered. "But it might have something to do with the fact that we're going ten miles an hour and the speed limit is forty."

"Turn here," Buffhunk said.

Screeech! The Jeep skidded to a halt. I lurched forward and crashed to the floor.

"I don't think you have to push so hard on the brakes," said Buffhunk, who was holding his nose where it had banged against the dashboard.

"Sorry," said Foxybabe. "I guess cars stop easier than they used to."

"It's called power brakes," grumbled Richgurl.

They really ought to make seat belts for dogs, I thought as I climbed back onto my seat.

Buffhunk picked up the map again. "We're going to make a right turn here and go down about half a block and then enter an underground garage."

The Jeep crawled down the street with the long line of cars creeping behind it, honking their horns loudly. Not exactly my idea of a secret mission. We went into the underground garage.

Screeech! Once again Foxybabe hit the brakes and we all flew forward.

"Sorry!" She patted her white hair nervously.

I got off the floor while Richgurl pushed open the door. Rarely have I been so glad to get out of a car. Following instructions left for us in the Jeep's glove compartment, we entered the building above the garage and took the elevator to the fourteenth floor.

"Oh, wow!" Buffhunk gasped as he opened the door to the apartment we would use as our base of operations. Richgurl, Foxybabe, and I followed him inside. We passed two tables lined with computers, printers, and fax machines. Just as Lassie had promised, a giant-size bag of rawhide bones lay in the corner.

The others looked around in wonder.

Woof! I barked, and pointed my nose toward a low glass coffee table with three chairs around it. We had more important things to do than stand around and admire the hardware.

"You want us to sit?" Richgurl asked.

Woof! I nodded.

"Well, this sure is different," Buffhunk chuckled. "When was the last time a dog told a human to sit?"

"Yeah," added Richgurl. "Talk about *Alice in Wonderland*."

They were nervous. I could smell it. Each of them sat down. I sat on the floor where the fourth chair would have been. The three of them kept giving one another uncomfortable glances.

Buffhunk cleared his throat. "So, uh, what now?"

Richgurl chewed on a nail and crossed her legs.

Foxybabe kept patting her white hair.

I sat there, studying them. Former high-level spies? They *had* to be kidding!

"Well?" Richgurl swung her leg nervously. "What's this powwow all about?"

"Er, I think I know," said Buffhunk. "I mean, we're not exactly what we pretended to be in the chat room, are we?"

Foxybabe pointed a finger at me. "Neither is he."

Grrrrrrr! I growled angrily.

"Byte never said he was human," Buffhunk pointed out. "We just assumed he was."

"He said he was a former agent," said Foxybabe.

Arf! I nodded.

"Give me a break," Richgurl snorted. "Since when does the government use dogs as spies?"

Grrrrrrr!

"Hey!" Richgurl yelped. "I'm just being honest."

"The AIA," Buffhunk mumbled.

"The what?" Foxybabe wrinkled her forehead, which wasn't easy since she was already pretty wrinkled.

"The Animal Intelligence Agency," Buffhunk explained. "Ultra top secret. You'd hear people whisper about it, but you never knew for sure that it really existed."

"What did it do?" Richgurl asked.

"Animals were genetically modified for superior intelligence," Buffhunk explained. "Dolphins for underwater missions. Chimpanzees for jungle work. Dogs were used mostly in domestic operations."

"Why use animals?" Foxybabe asked. "Why not stick with humans?"

Buffhunk took a deep breath and let it out slowly. "They were used for missions considered too dangerous for humans. Missions where they weren't expected to survive."

"That's terrible!" Richgurl cried.

"They were trained for operations where the government thought they'd die?" Foxybabe asked.

Buffhunk nodded.

"Oh, Byte." Richgurl reached down and stroked my head. "That's so cruel."

I held my chin up. We in the AIA knew the risks and served our country proudly. If you wanted to be a bleeding heart liberal you could join the ASPCA.

"If the AIA could genetically engineer these animals to be so smart, why couldn't it teach them to talk?" Foxybabe asked.

"The AIA didn't want them to talk," Buffhunk explained. "That way, if they were captured and tortured, they couldn't reveal government secrets."

"Oh, dear," Foxybabe gasped. "That's terribly cruel."

The room grew quiet. The three of them gave me concerned, sympathetic looks. Buffhunk heaved a sigh. "I owe you an apology, Byte. You recruited me because I pretended I was a high-level operative. But the truth is, the only thing I ever did in the CIA was dog work in the mail room. I got fired for sleeping on the job because I used to stay up all night talking in chat rooms. I don't know what you hoped I could do on this mission, but I probably can't do it."

"I guess I should apologize, too," Foxybabe said with a giggle. "Sorry, it's just that I've never apologized to a dog before. But I wasn't a code breaker at the NSA. I was just a secretary."

The three of us looked at Richgurl, who shrugged. "It's pretty obvious I never even worked in the government. My dad did."

"Which agency?" Buffhunk asked.

"The FBI. He was a mechanic in the motor pool until he cracked up one of their cars."

"That doesn't sound fair," Foxybabe said. "I mean, accidents happen."

"It was at a stock car race," Richgurl said.

"He entered an FBI car in a stock car race?" Buffhunk asked in disbelief.

"Don't knock it," Richgurl snarled. "He was in second place when he crashed."

I cocked my head, still puzzled.

"So you're wondering what I was doing in your chat room in the first place?" Richgurl guessed. "Look, I'm fourteen, okay? You ever hang out in a teenage chat room? If you think we made stuff up, you won't believe what goes on in those rooms. I just got tired of all the shaggy dog stories. You guys sounded a lot more mature."

The others slowly turned and looked at me.

"I guess we all let you down, Byte," Buffhunk said. "It sounds like you've got a serious mission on your hands, er, I mean, on your *paws*. We're probably the last bunch of losers you need."

Buffhunk was right. They probably were the last bunch of losers I needed on this mission. But it was too late. I got up and trotted over to the table with the computers. I hopped onto a chair in front of one of the computers and started to type. The others stood behind me and watched.

"Hee, hee, hee." Foxybabe started to giggle again. "Sorry! I just can't believe I'm watching a dog type!"

I typed: We have a mission to do and we're the only ones who can do it.

"Can't you find someone more qualified?" Buffhunk asked.

No time, I typed.

"How are we going to do it?" Richgurl asked.

Buffhunk stays here and runs the computer communications link, I typed. Foxybabe does surveillance from the car while Richgurl and I sniff out the bad guys.

"But there are thousands of places where dogs aren't allowed," Richgurl pointed out. "How are we going to do it?"

Undercover, I typed.

A little while later Richgurl and I hit the streets. Foxybabe followed in the Jeep.

"I have to admit it, Byte," Richgurl said as she adjusted her sunglasses. "This is a stroke of genius."

Arf! I barked in agreement.

Richgurl reached down and grabbed the handle of the guide-dog harness I was wearing. With Richgurl pretending to be blind, there was practically no place I couldn't go.

It being the week between Christmas and New Year's, the sidewalks in the capital weren't as crowded as normal. Some businesspeople in dark suits passed us, talking on cell phones. Other people lugged shopping bags filled with Christmas gifts to be returned. Families of tourists wandered past, clutching guidebooks. Richgurl and I moved along as fast as possible without attracting attention. We didn't have much time and there was a lot of territory to cover.

For a normal dog, all the scents of the city might have been distracting. But I was no average canine. I'd been genetically engineered to sniff out the most microscopic scents imaginable. The scent of that terrorist letter was imprinted in my brain. All I had to do was keep my head down and my nose focused.

The air of the capital was filled with a thousand different smells. I have to admit that I was excited. Despite all the bitterness I felt about what the AIA had done to me, it was good to be working on a mission again.

"Oh, what a cute dog," someone suddenly said.

Richgurl would have kept walking, but I recognized the scent and stopped. It was Lassie, dressed in a meter maid's outfit! She gave me a puzzled look, darting her eyes at Richgurl.

I knew what she was thinking. I'd told her I'd gather a top-notch team of former agents for this mission. She had to be wondering who this fourteen-year-old girl with the purple hair and dog collar was.

I gave Lassie a slight nod to let her know that I understood what was worrying her. A moment later, Richgurl and I were once again heading down the sidewalk. I had no doubt that I'd hear from Lassie again. And soon.

Richgurl and I passed stores and businesses. With each sniff I sorted through a thousand different bits of smell in the air. At times it could get confusing. I had to keep my head down and concentrate. Somewhere in that rich soup of scents might be the single trace that we needed to crack this case.

Suddenly Richgurl pulled back on my harness. I looked up to see what the matter was. Richgurl had stopped beside the window of a shop. A big red sign in the window said: HOLIDAY SALE.

Inside were all sorts of black leather jackets and belts with silver studs.

Richgurl was staring through the window at them!

I pulled back to get her attention.

She was so distracted by the window that she let go of the harness!

I couldn't believe it! She'd completely forgotten what she was supposed to be doing! We were on a mission! And she was supposed to be blind!

Grrrrr! I growled.

Richgurl looked down at me with a frown on her face. I jerked my head forward.

"Can't I just take a second to look?" she asked.

I twisted my head around to the guide-dog harness.

"I know I'm supposed to be blind," Richgurl said. "But I never get to see shops like this."

Unbelievable! I thought. The future of our country was at stake and she wanted to window-shop?

Not only that, but people on the sidewalk were

starting to notice that the girl with the sun-glasses and the guide dog was looking into the window.

Grrrrr! I growled again. Didn't she realize she was blowing our cover?

"Just chill out a second," Richgurl grumbled.

This was unacceptable! With no intention of letting this mission go to the dogs, I turned away and headed back to the apartment.

A few minutes later I used my head to push open the glass doors of the apartment building. In the elevator I got up on my hind legs to push the elevator button. On the fourteenth floor I scratched on the apartment door.

"Who is it?" Buffhunk called from inside.

Ruff! I barked.

A moment later the door swung open. Buffhunk looked surprised.

"Byte, what are you doing here?" he asked as I marched across the living room and sat at one of the computers.

Richgurl is blowing the mission, I typed angrily.

"How?" Buffhunk asked as he read over my shoulder.

Window-shopping, I typed.

Just then the apartment door opened. Richgurl came in with a real hangdog look on her face. Foxybabe followed her.

"What's with you?" Richgurl asked.

64

260 million people in this country are depending on you! I typed.

"Aw, come on, that's not fair!" Richgurl whined.

This is an important mission, I typed. If you can't take it seriously, you shouldn't be here.

"But I never get to the city," Richgurl complained. "The stores where I live are completely lame."

This is a matter of national security, I typed.

I might have expected more arguments from Richgurl, but the last thing I expected was what Buffhunk asked next: "If it's so important, how come we're the only ones assigned to it?"

I thought I explained that, I typed. Every other available agent has been assigned to another mission.

The three of them shared an uncertain look.

"Listen, Byte." Foxybabe stroked my head. "We know you think this is very serious, but it's hard to imagine the government assigning something so important to a dog. I think I'm speaking for all of us when I say that we're willing to work with you, but you should be willing to work with us, too. It's after Christmas. Things are on sale and dog cheap. If one of us wants to look in a few stores, I don't think it can hurt."

I couldn't believe it! My team was disobeying me!

"Uh, Byte?" Buffhunk had moved over to another computer. "I think you better see this."

I jumped down from my chair and had a look. It was an Instant Message:

URGENT!
Byte — Go to the garage ASAP. Alone!
— Lassie

TUESDAY, DECEMBER 28, 1999
1645 HRS

I left the apartment and headed downstairs. A man and woman in the elevator gave me a funny look, but I just stood there and stared straight ahead. I didn't press the button for the garage until they got out in the lobby.

The underground garage was filled with cars but strangely quiet. I could hear water dripping somewhere. I perked my ears and felt my fur go up.

It was too quiet.

I stood still and listened for a long time.

What was going on?

Why had Lassie called me to meet her here?

What if it was a trick?

Suddenly I heard the softest padding of paws on the ground.

I spun around.

A cat was trotting toward me. Calico-colored, orange, white, and black.

I watched carefully. One thing you learn in the

spy business is that nothing is what it appears to be.

The cat sauntered along, not even giving me a look. Just as she passed, she gave her head the slightest jerk. It was a signal that she wanted me to follow.

I waited a moment and then made a beeline for the feline. The cat doubled back and started out of the garage and onto the sidewalk. We'd hardly gone more than a dozen yards when she turned into an alley.

Uh-oh. I hesitated before going farther. Alleys were classic ambush territory. The cat looked back over her shoulder at me and nodded, urging me to keep up.

I stepped carefully into the alley. Suddenly things began to happen fast. The calico cat jumped up on a garbage can and then vaulted over a tall wooden fence and disappeared.

At the same moment, a city sanitation truck backed into the alley.

I was trapped. Blocked at one end of the alley by the wooden fence and at the other end by the sanitation truck. My heart began to bang against my ribs and my mouth went dry.

Someone wearing a dark green sanitation uniform and matching cap jumped down from the truck. I had good reason to suspect that whoever it was, he wasn't a garbageman.

I braced myself, ready to fight.

Suddenly a familiar scent hit my nose just as a wisp of red hair fell out from under the cap. I relaxed. It was Lassie.

"Didn't mean to scare you," she said.

I shrugged it off as if it were nothing. Meanwhile, my heart was still pounding.

"What did you think of the cat?" Lassie asked.

I nodded. It was a nice touch. There hadn't been any cats in the AIA when I was there.

"We're training her for indoor work," Lassie explained. "Cat and mouse stuff."

It made sense.

"I checked on your team," she said. "A former CIA mail room clerk who was canned for sleeping on the job. A retired NSA secretary. And a fourteen-year-old kid whose father was let go from the FBI after confusing the arms race with the Daytona 500. I thought you said this would be a crackerjack team, Byte."

I shrugged.

"I understand that you met them in a private chat room," Lassie went on. "Guess it just proves that you can't believe what anyone says in those rooms."

I nodded and gave her a curious look.

"You want to know if I've got any more information," Lassie guessed. "There's a little, but I'm afraid it's not much. My friend in the lab traced some of the type in the terrorist's letter to a trade publication called *Modern Toilet*."

I scowled at her.

"Trade publications are the magazines people in certain businesses read," Lassie explained. "If you own a restaurant, you read *Restaurant Weekly*. If you run a Laundromat, there's *Laundromat World*. All we know is that the person who wrote that letter *may* have something to do with toilets. The trouble is, we don't know what. Do they make them? Sell them? Fix them? Anything's possible."

I nodded. At least it was a lead. I gave her another curious look. Was there anything else?

"My friend in the NSA is keeping an eye out for any sign of unusual activities having to do with toilets," Lassie promised. "But for now, that's all you have to go on."

TUESDAY, DECEMBER 28, 1999
1700 HRS

B ack in the apartment I shared the news with the rest of the team. We had a terrorist letter from a mysterious organization named PHLUSH demanding a billion dollars and the use of the Lincoln Memorial. And now we knew that some of the type from the letter had come from a trade publication called *Modern Toilet*.

"Plumbers," Buffhunk mumbled and picked up a phone book.

"What are you doing?" asked Richgurl.

"Checking the address of every plumber and plumbing supply store in the capital," Buffhunk said.

"You really think a bunch of plumbers is behind this?" Foxybabe asked.

"I'm saying it's possible," answered Buffhunk.

"How could plumbers bring our country to a halt?" asked Richgurl. "And what would they want with the Lincoln Memorial?"

"I don't know yet," answered Buffhunk. "But at least it's a lead."

"I think it's the dumbest thing I ever heard," said Foxybabe. "My sixth husband was a plumber."

"How many did you have?" Richgurl asked.

"Plumbers or husbands?" replied Foxybabe.

"Husbands," said Richgurl.

"Ten, but I would have been better off with a good plumber."

Woof! I barked. They were getting off the track.

"What do you think, Byte?" asked Richgurl. "Should we follow the plumbing lead or are we barking up the wrong tree?"

I winced. I knew the pun was unintentional, but still. . . . On the other hand, Richgurl's question was a good one. The idea of a group of renegade plumbers trying to bring down our country sounded pretty strange. But Buffhunk was also right. It was our only lead.

Arf! I nodded.

"All right," Richgurl said. "Starting tomorrow, we focus the investigation on plumbers."

FROM TUESDAY, DECEMBER 28, TO
WEDNESDAY, DECEMBER 29, 1999

For the next twenty-four hours Foxybabe, Richgurl, and I sniffed around all the plumbing establishments in the capital. But like so many missions in the world of espionage, what started out as a promising lead slowly went nowhere. We failed to turn up a single clue.

There were a few tantalizing but frustrating moments. Once, near a construction site, I was certain I picked up the same scent I'd smelled on the terrorist's letter. But there was no way to investigate it. The last place in the world a blind person, even with a guide dog, would be allowed was a construction site.

Foxybabe took digital photos of the site and later we went over them carefully. But all we saw were some trucks and bulldozers and a bunch of construction workers digging a big hole in the ground.

Another time I thought I caught a whiff near a

highway overpass that was blocked off while a road crew repaired it. Once again, Foxybabe shot the area digitally. She was good with the camera and remembered to zoom in on the human. But once again we found nothing.

WEDNESDAY, DECEMBER 29, 1999
2100 HRS

It was Wednesday night at 9 o'clock. A little more than forty-eighty hours until New Year's Eve. After another long day of frustration and another fast-food meal, we gathered around the coffee table.

Yesterday the coffee table was clean. Now it was covered with used Chinese food containers, empty pizza boxes, and dog-eared paperbacks.

Foxybabe cleared her throat loudly. "Ahem!"

We all looked up.

"I hate to say this, folks," she said, "but New Year's Eve is the day after tomorrow. I think we've all served our country well, but maybe it's time to pack it in and go home for the big celebration."

I'd been afraid one of them would say that. Meanwhile, neither Richgurl nor Buffhunk would look me in the eye. I got up and went over to the computer and started to type. The others read over my shoulder.

Do the rest of you feel that way? I typed.

"I never thought I'd hear myself say this," said Richgurl, "but I'm getting tired of pizza and Chinese food."

I knew how she felt. I was even getting tired of those rawhide bones.

"We've been searching nonstop and we still haven't come up with one solid clue," added Buffhunk.

I began to type. The fut —

"Don't give us that saving-the-country stuff again, Byte," Foxybabe said. "That's all we've heard for almost two days."

"It is starting to wear thin," Richgurl admitted.

"I mean, suppose there really is a PHLUSH?" Foxybabe asked. "What makes you think we've got a dog's chance of finding them?"

They were both right. Even Lassie had admitted that her superiors thought the letter from PHLUSH was a joke. What if they were right and Lassie was wrong?

Okay, I typed. Let's give it one more day. If we don't have anything by tomorrow night, this mission is over. You can fly out Friday morning and be home in time for New Year's Eve.

THURSDAY, DECEMBER 30, 1999
0600 Hrs

"I can't believe this," Richgurl groaned when we set out the next morning. "It's practically the middle of the night!"

She was exaggerating. It was six A.M. The sun was just starting to rise over the Capitol. Joggers wearing headphones passed us on the sidewalk. Trucks carrying newspapers rumbled down the street.

"Being a dog, you probably don't know this," Richgurl said as we passed rows of closed stores, "but it's been scientifically proven that teenagers have a different sleeping pattern than other people. We're supposed to sleep late and stay up late."

Suddenly she yanked on the harness and stopped.

Oh, no! I thought. *Not another holiday sale in leather goods!*

But there was no store window. Just a wall with a small poster pasted to it.

"You better see this, Byte," Richgurl said.

I stood on my back feet and put my forepaws against the wall. The poster had a picture of me on it:

LOST DOG   BIG REWARD

BYTE

Please help us find Byte, our
yellow Labrador retriever.
Byte is 8 years old and
weighs about 90 pounds. He is
missing half of his left ear. He was
last seen wearing a black dog
collar. We love him and miss
him. Finding him would make this the
best New Year's Eve ever.
— The Barkleys

I felt a tug at my heart and a lump in my throat. The Barkleys! I'd almost forgotten about them! But they sure hadn't forgotten about me! That made me feel bad. My job was to protect them, not make them worry.

Richgurl tipped up her sunglasses and gave me a concerned look. "You okay, Byte?"

Huh? Of course I was okay. I'd been trained. I knew the cost of freedom was high. It was a dog-eat-dog world, and this was our mission. National security was at stake. Sometimes people were called upon to sacrifice for the sake of their country. Dogs, too.

Arf! I gave her a good, solid bark. It was time to get back to work.

We hit the pavement again. During the next few hours we covered as many plumbers and plumbing supply shops as we could. A lot of them smelled bad, but not one of them smelled right.

In the meantime, we passed three more posters put up by the Barkleys. Each time I saw one, I felt more choked up. There seemed to be posters all over the city. Benjy must have been heart-broken. In the meantime I was off chasing what might be a practical joke.

THURSDAY, DECEMBER 30, 1999
1630 HRS

It was late afternoon. Richgurl and I had been trudging along nonstop for more than ten hours. After three straight days, my paws were sore and my mouth was dry. Today the sidewalks were filled with shoppers carrying bags of party hats, streamers, and balloons. Banners exclaiming HAPPY NEW YEAR! were hanging in store windows and we could hear distant bangs and pops as overeager celebrators set off early fireworks.

Richgurl pulled on my harness and stopped. "I hate to say this, Byte, but with all this New Year's Eve stuff, I'm starting to miss the old trailer park. Every year Old Man Pointer puts on a fireworks display. I bet this year he's planning the best ever."

Arf! And I missed the Barkleys. Every cloud has a silver lining. We might fail in our mission to find the terrorists, but it would be nice to get home.

Screech! A black stretch limo skidded to a stop on the street beside us. A door swung open. In the shadows inside sat Lassie.

"Get in," she said.

Richgurl pulled back on my harness. "Mom told me never to accept a ride from a stranger."

"I'm not a stranger," Lassie said from inside the limo.

"I don't know you," said Richgurl. "Our family rule is you don't get in a car with anyone who hasn't eaten dinner at your house."

Lassie turned to the driver of the limo. "Put her in, Rex."

In a flash the driver jumped out and shoved Richgurl into the back of the limo. I jumped in, and Rex slammed the door behind me. Richgurl instantly reached for the door and tried to open it.

"Why won't it open?" she cried as Rex got back into the driver's seat and the limo pulled away from the curb.

"It's locked from the outside," Lassie calmly explained.

Richgurl yanked on the door again. "I've never heard of a car with doors that locked from the outside."

"Welcome to the AIA," said Lassie.

THURSDAY, DECEMBER 30, 1999
1700 HRS

R ichgurl sank back into the seat.
"Am I being kidnapped?" she asked.

"I'm taking you to headquarters," Lassie explained, taking out a black cloth. "There's been a new development in the case. Put this on."

Richgurl took the cloth. "It's kind of small for a scarf."

"That's because it's a blindfold," said Lassie. "You'll have to wear it until we're inside."

Twenty minutes later we arrived at AIA headquarters. Inside, Lassie led us into a small darkened room with two chairs facing a large two-way mirror. On the other side of the mirror a man wearing a greasy dark blue jumpsuit sat alone at a table.

"Is that really a two-way mirror?" Richgurl asked as she took a seat.

"Shush!" Lassie hissed. "He can't see us, but he can hear us. Just have a seat and watch."

"Wow," Richgurl whispered as she sat down.

"I didn't think these things really existed."

"Hush!" Lassie whispered, then left the room.

The man in the room on the other side of the mirror glanced around nervously. Suddenly the door opened and Lassie entered.

"Who are you?" the man asked. "You can't hold me against my will. I haven't done anything wrong. I want a lawyer."

Lassie calmly sat down in a chair on the other side of the table. "Let me explain, Mr. Bassett. You are being held as a material witness under the Domestic Antiterrorism Act."

"Terrorism?" Mr. Bassett repeated. "I don't know what you're talking about."

"Perhaps you'd like to tell me why federal agents found a semitrailer full of toilet paper this morning in the parking lot behind your office," Lassie said.

A tiny muscle under Mr. Bassett's left eye started to twitch.

"I don't have to tell you," he said.

"Have you ever heard of Dog Island, Mr. Bassett?" Lassie asked. "It's a tiny, mosquito-infested island off the coast of Florida. It's where the government sends domestic terrorists."

Mr. Bassett's eye twitched faster. He swallowed nervously. "Okay, okay. You want to know why I was stockpiling toilet paper? It's because of this Y2K thing. Everybody's been stockpiling stuff."

"Mr. Bassett, there were approximately 450,000 rolls of toilet paper in that trailer," Lassie said.

"What can I tell you?" Mr. Bassett shrugged. "I use a lot of toilet paper."

"Even at the rate of one roll a day, it would take you approximately 1,232 years to use that many rolls," Lassie replied calmly.

"Maybe I use more than a roll a day," Mr. Bassett replied defiantly. "Maybe I like to wrap myself up in it every night like a mummy."

Lassie narrowed her eyes. "Did I mention that it often hits 110 degrees on Dog Island and that prisoners of domestic terrorism have to use an outhouse?"

Small beads of sweat began to appear on Mr. Bassett's forehead. His left eye was twitching like crazy.

"Okay, okay," he said. "Maybe I didn't plan to use all that toilet paper myself. Maybe I planned to sell some of it."

"Why?" Lassie asked.

"Like I said, people are gonna need a lot of stuff when this Y2K thing hits," Mr. Bassett said.

"Why would you think that?" Lassie asked. "We're almost certain that all the major computer systems in the country have been corrected for Y2K. There may be some minor glitches here and there, but that's it. What do you know that we don't know?"

Mr. Bassett's eyes began to dart left and right. Small trails of sweat had begun to trickle down his forehead. Lassie leaned forward.

"Dog Island is a long way from anywhere, Mr. Bassett," she said. "And once you're there it's too late to change your mind."

Drops of sweat dripped off Mr. Bassett's nose and chin. "Look, I don't know anything, okay? I'm telling you the truth. You just hear stuff."

Lassie leaned closer. "What kind of stuff?"

"Just rumors, you know? That something big's gonna go down at midnight on New Year's Eve," Mr. Bassett said. "Something that's gonna plug up the whole country. Clog it up good. I mean, bring it straight to its knees."

"But why stock up on toilet paper, Mr. Bassett?" Lassie asked.

"Because," Mr. Bassett answered, "from what I hear, that's the one thing everyone's going to be screaming for."

Mr. Bassett insisted that was all he knew. A few minutes later, Lassie called two uniformed guards to take him away.

"You're not sending me to that island, are you?" Mr. Bassett cried as the guards dragged him out of the room. "I swear I don't know nothing! You gotta believe me!"

A few moments later Lassie joined Richgurl and me in the room behind the two-way mirror.

"You're not really going to send him to Dog Island, are you?" Richgurl asked.

Lassie shook her head. "Toledo, maybe. But just to give him a little scare in case he really does know more. In the meantime, clearly Mr. Bassett expects the price of toilet paper to sky-rocket."

"Why?" Richgurl asked.

"Hard to say," Lassie answered. "It could be a plan to put some kind of chemical agent into the water supply that will cause upset stomachs nationwide. We're checking into that. We've also had reports of stolen shipments of Redi-Wipes and diapers. Some of us think those things might be related to Mr. Bassett's interest in toilet paper."

I sat up on my haunches and pretended I was typing.

"Gotcha, Byte." Lassie left the room and returned a moment later with a laptop computer.

How about a plan to sabotage toilet-paper manufacturers? I typed.

"We've considered that," Lassie said. "We're beefing up security at most of the major toilet-paper manufacturing facilities."

"I'm sorry," said Richgurl, "but it doesn't sound right to me. I mean, so what if they shut down the toilet-paper makers? You can always get by with tissues in a pinch. I mean, there've been times when I've even used paper napkins."

"Ahem." Lassie cleared her throat. "Thanks for sharing that with us. I think you've made a good point. There are hundreds of possibilities. The problem is, if PHLUSH *isn't* putting a stomach-upsetting agent in the water, and it's not attacking the makers of toilet paper, then what is it up to?"

Later that night, Foxybabe opened the apartment door with a concerned look on her face.

"What happened to you two?" she asked. "One moment you were on the sidewalk. And the next you were gone! I thought you'd been kidnapped."

"We were," replied Richgurl.

"By who?" asked Buffhunk.

Richgurl told them how we'd been taken to AIA headquarters to watch the interrogation of the toilet-paper hoarder. And about the reports of people hoarding large quantities of wipes and diapers as well.

"A terrorist organization that calls itself PHLUSH and may involve plumbers," Buffhunk mused. "People hoarding toilet paper, wipes, and diapers. It could be related."

"Or maybe it's not," argued Foxybabe. "People are hoarding all sorts of things. You said you were hoarding food and water, Buff. My point is, maybe it's time to let sleeping dogs lie. Byte said we could leave tomorrow morning so that we'd be home in time for New Year's Eve tomorrow night."

I gazed at Buffhunk and Richgurl.

"You want to go over to the computer and tell us what you're thinking?" Buffhunk asked me.

"He doesn't have to," Richgurl said. "I'm pretty sure I know. You're hoping we'll stick with you a little longer. Right, Byte?"

Arf! I nodded.

"But he said—" Foxybabe began to argue.

"Yes, he did," Richgurl cut her short. "But that was before we got this latest information. Maybe you're right, Foxy, maybe there's nothing to it. Or maybe it really is something big, and if we don't find it, this country's going to be in deep . . . er, trouble. But there's something else I found out today. You think you have a good reason for going home, Foxy. But none of us has as good a reason for going home as Byte."

She told them about the posters we'd seen all over town that day and how obvious it was that the Barkleys were heartbroken thinking I'd run away or been dognapped. And how their New Year's Eve was going to be ruined if I didn't make it home.

Foxybabe turned to me with watery eyes. "That's so sad, Byte. They love you. And yet, you're still willing to stay tomorrow?"

Yip. I nodded.

"Well, I don't know about the rest of you, but if Byte's willing to stay, then I'm willing to stay, too," said Buffhunk. "Truth is, I didn't have any plans for New Year's anyway. I probably would have spent it watching Austin Powers movies."

I turned to Richgurl.

"I'm with you, too, Byte," she said. "I can always catch Old Man Pointer's fireworks next year."

We all turned to Foxybabe.

"Oh, heck!" she grumbled. "All right. I'll stay, too. New Year's at the home probably won't be so great anyway. Most of those old geezers can't keep their eyes open past nine o'clock."

Richgurl looked at her watch. "I hate to say this, but it's a little after seven o'clock. That gives us less than seventeen hours until the terrorists' deadline of noon tomorrow. If we're going to find those guys, we better get moving."

Ruff! I shook my head and trotted over to the computer. The others followed.

We don't have time to go back to the streets, I typed. We have to use our brains to figure this out. PHLUSH says it's going to shut down the United States. That <u>must</u> mean they plan to attack a major support system that everyone relies on.

"But the government says they've checked every major system," Foxybabe pointed out.

There has to be one they've overlooked, I

typed. And the only way to solve this case is to figure out which one it is.

"Byte is right," Buffhunk said. "Until we know how PHLUSH intends to cripple the country, there's no way we can begin to stop it. Now, if you'll excuse me, I need to use the bathroom."

Buffhunk started out of the room.

"Wait!" Richgurl suddenly cried.

Buff stopped. "What?"

"That's it!" Richgurl jumped up and started to hug Buffhunk with joy.

"What's it?" Buffhunk asked.

"What's with her?" asked Foxybabe.

Woof! Woof! I barked at Richgurl. *Tell us!*

But Richgurl was too busy hugging Buffhunk. "I can't believe it! You're a genius! You figured it out!"

"I did?" Buffhunk said.

"Yes!" cried Richgurl.

"All I said was I had to use the bathroom," Buffhunk said.

"Yes!" Richgurl shouted and hugged him some more.

"Hey! Easy! Easy!" Buffhunk cried. "Don't squeeze so hard!"

"Come on, tell us what's going on," Foxybabe pleaded.

"I'll tell you what's going on," said Buffhunk. "If I don't get to the bathroom soon I'm gonna have a big problem."

Richgurl let go of Buffhunk and took a few breaths to calm herself. "Okay, guys. You were right. There's one system the government hasn't checked. And if it's ever shut down, the whole country will be paralyzed."

"What system is it?" Foxybabe asked.

"Don't keep us guessing," Buffhunk gasped. "I really gotta go bad!"

"Not as bad as if PHLUSH succeeds," Richgurl assured him.

"Okay, guys," Richgurl said. "It's . . . the sewer system."

"Oh, my gosh!" Buffhunk cried. "Of course! If they shut down the sewer system all the toilets will back up! Just imagine it! By noon on New Year's Day every toilet in the country will be clogged up. In every home, in every school, in every business, in every government building, in every gas station. Not a single toilet will work!"

"There'll be total panic," Richgurl predicted.

"Mayhem," added Foxybabe.

"Excuse me," Buffhunk said. "But now I'm *really* gonna use that bathroom."

Buffhunk hurried off.

Woof! I barked.

"What is it, Byte?" Richgurl asked.

Woof! Woof! I cocked my head and gave her a puzzled look.

"You don't understand what's so bad about

every toilet in the country backing up?" Foxy-babe guessed.

I nodded.

"Oh, Byte." Richgurl rubbed my head. "You may be brilliant. But you're still a dog."

Grrrrrr! I snarled. I hated it when humans were condescending.

"You'll just have to believe me," Richgurl said. "Unlike your species, we humans can't exist without working toilets."

"But I still don't understand how PHLUSH can do that," Foxybabe said.

"I do," said Buffhunk as he returned from the bathroom. "Almost every sewer system in this country is connected to some kind of waste treatment plant. Just about every town and city has one. And just like everything else, those waste treatment plants depend on computers. So it's easy. PHLUSH has probably already hacked into the computers that run the sewage treatment plants. They've probably already planted their Y2K bugs. Now they're just waiting until tomorrow. If their demands aren't met by noon they'll get on their computers and activate those bugs."

A moment of silence passed. I think we were all stunned by the realization that it really *could* happen. The entire United States brought to a halt. Two hundred seventy million people in a complete panic, with only one thing on their minds: *To Find a Working Toilet!*

96

Richgurl wrinkled her nose. "Yuck!"

"What can we do?" Foxybabe asked.

"There's only one thing we can do!" Buffhunk hurried to the computer. "Come on, everyone, get on a computer. We have to hack into the city sewer system and find that bug."

THURSDAY, DECEMBER 30, 1999
2200 HRS

It was dark outside. The four of us sat at our computers, searching through cyberspace for evidence of PHLUSH's sewer bug. We must have looked like an unlikely bunch. A wrinkled old white-haired lady in a miniskirt. A punky teenager with purple hair, tattoos, and a dog collar. A bald and bearded chubster. And a dog.

Long into the night we stared at our computer screens, searching for that one bug that would confirm our theory.

Hour after hour passed.

The clock ticked, 12:01 A.M. It was now Friday, December 31, 1999. The last day of the millennium. Possibly the last day of civilization as we knew it.

Around two A.M. Foxybabe slid her chair back and yawned. "I hate to say it, guys, but I'm pooped."

Richgurl wrinkled her nose. "No offense, Foxy, but considering what we're up against, do you think you could find another way of saying it?"

"Sorry," Foxybabe said. "I've got to get some shut-eye. I'll start again first thing in the morning."

Around three A.M. Buffhunk rubbed his eyes and shook his head. "I'm dog tired."

I winced.

Buffhunk saw me. "Ooops! Sorry, Byte. All I meant was, I gotta get some rest."

About an hour later, Richgurl shut down her computer and turned to me. "My head's pounding. I don't even know what I'm looking at anymore. I'm sorry, Byte. Maybe if I just take a catnap I'll be okay."

Arf. I understood. My eyes were hurting, too. You could push a body just so far.

"You'll keep trying?" Richgurl asked with a yawn as she got up.

I nodded. But the truth was, I didn't know how much longer I could go, either.

FRIDAY, DECEMBER 31, 1999
0600 HRS

*K*nock! Knock!* I jerked my head up as the loud rap of knuckles against the apartment door woke me with a start. I realized I'd fallen asleep with my head on the computer keyboard. The screen looked like this:

yyyyyyyyyyyyyyyyyyyyyyyyyyyyyyyyyyyyyyyyyyy
yyyyyyyyyyyyyyyyyyyyyyyyyyyyyyyyyyyyyyyyyyy
yyyyyyyyyyyyyyyyyyyyyyyyyyyyyyyyyyyyyyyyyyy
yyyyyyyyyyyyyyyyyyyyyyyyyyyyyyyyyyyyyyyyyyy
yyyyyyyyyyyyyyyyyyyyyyyyyyyyyyyyyyyyyyyyyyy
yyyyyyyyyyyyyyyyyyyyyyyyyyyyyyyyyyyyyyyyyyy
yyyyyyyyyyyyyyyyyyyyyyyyyyyyyyyyyyyyyyyyyyy
yyyyyyyyyyyyyyyyyyyyyyyyyyyyyyyyyyyyyyyyyyy
yyyyyyyyyyyyyyyyyyyyyyyyyyyyyyyyyyyyyyyyyyy
yyyyyyyyyyyyyyyyyyyyyyyyyyyyyyyyyyyyyyyyyyy
yyyyyyyyyyyyyyyyyyyyyyyyyyyyyyyyyyyyyyyyyyy
yyyyyyyyyyyyyyyyyyyyy

Knock! Knock! Whoever was out there was hitting the door hard. I couldn't imagine who it could be. As I got up and stretched, I looked around. Buffhunk was asleep on the couch. I assumed Foxybabe and Richgurl were in the bedrooms.

Knock! Knock! The knocking woke Buffhunk. He stared at me with bleary eyes.

"Who?" he whispered.

Crash! The apartment door smashed down and four burly thugs wearing dark green jumpsuits burst into the room.

They were followed by a thin man with blond hair and thick glasses. He bore an uncanny resemblance to Bill Gates. Suddenly the scent from the terrorist letter was everywhere.

"Grab them!" the blond-haired man ordered.

"What about the mutt?" one of the thugs asked.

"Him, too," said the man. "And get those computers. We're taking it all."

My friends were handcuffed and blindfolded. Their mouths were taped shut. I was blindfolded, muzzled, and hooked to a choke chain. Our kidnappers were silent as they took us down in the elevator. I sensed that this was no dog and pony show. They were professionals.

I felt terrible. It was my fault that we'd been caught. I'd been so eager to track down the sewer bug that I'd forgotten to disguise our cybersearch. Clearly PHLUSH had been monitoring the computer systems. Once they detected us, it was easy for them to trace us back to the apartment.

From the echoes of their footsteps and the smell of motor oil, I knew they'd taken us into the underground garage. A van door slid open and I recognized the scent of the terrorist letter again. Oddly, I could tell now that it was partly perfume.

"Step up," one of the kidnappers grunted.

A moment later we were in the back of the van. The door was slammed shut and we were on the move.

The kidnappers didn't say a word as they drove. From the sound of their breathing I knew there were two of them in the front. The other two and the blond-haired man must've gotten into a second car.

We drove for nearly an hour, yet from the number of sharp turns and doglegs the van made, I sensed that we were really just going around in circles within the city. It was an old spy trick. The kidnappers wanted to make us think they were taking us far away.

Finally, the drive ended. We were led across a sidewalk to an elevator in a building and taken upstairs.

When the elevator doors opened, the terrorist letter scent was stronger than ever. It was an odd mixture of fragrances like one might find in a home like the Barkleys'.

We were led into a hall. From the soft bounce of the thick carpeting under my paws, I knew this was a fancy place. Probably the executive suites of a large company.

I heard a door open. The man holding my leash tugged sharply. The choke chain tightened around my neck. I turned and went into what felt like a large office.

A door closed. The scents in here were overwhelming! Cinnamon, pine, lemon, strawberry, raspberry . . .

"Take off the blindfolds and untape their mouths," the blond-haired man ordered.

"What about the dog, Mr. Curr?" someone else asked.

"Take off the blindfold, but leave the muzzle on," said the blond-haired man. I now knew his name was Curr.

My blindfold came off. Suddenly I could see. I looked around. As I'd suspected, I was in a large office.

But it was unlike any office I'd ever seen before.

The office was the size of a large living room. There were brown leather couches and comfortable chairs, as well as a broad wooden desk where Mr. Curr was sitting. Paintings hung on the walls and the shelves were filled with books. Along the wall behind us were lots of big windows. We must have been high up because all I could see was blue sky.

Two things made the office strange. The first was the dozens of scented candles burning on the desk and shelves, as well as the pink and blue plastic air fresheners stuck to the walls.

Stranger still were the things that looked like free-standing closets. I could recall seeing similar things at construction sites.

Some were old and square and made of wood. Others looked new and were made of bright blue or yellow or orange plastic. They were all about as tall as a man. And they all had narrow doors in them.

Many smaller models of these things lined the shelves of the office and even stood on Mr. Curr's desk.

Three full-size light blue versions of these things were lined up in front of Mr. Curr's desk. Buffhunk, Foxybabe, and Richgurl were each sitting handcuffed in one of them. The doors were open so that Mr. Curr could see them from his desk.

The man holding my leash kept me off to the side where I could see both Mr. Curr and my friends.

"What is this?" Buffhunk asked with a frown from inside his light blue cell.

"What's that smell?" asked Foxybabe.

"I'll ask the questions, thank you," Mr. Curr replied coldly. "First of all, what do you know?"

Buffhunk, Foxybabe, and Richgurl said nothing. They couldn't see one another, but they all glanced at me.

Woof! I barked and quickly shook my head.

Mr. Curr nodded. "Very interesting."

Now he stared at me. I immediately went into my "dumb dog" act, sitting up and panting with my tongue hanging out.

"Nice try, Fido," Mr. Curr said with a smirk. He turned to the others. "Let's not be silly, shall we? You know I can make you talk."

I felt a surge of pride as my team remained tight-lipped. Whatever Mr. Curr wanted, he was going to find out that we were a lot tougher than he thought.

Mr. Curr narrowed his eyes at us and then turned to one of the big burly men wearing the dark green jumpsuits.

"They don't seem to believe me, Duke," he said. "Please take out the tools."

The man named Duke opened a closet and took out a dark canvas bag. He unzipped it and started to remove the most frightening collection of torture instruments I'd ever seen. My heart began to pound and my mouth went dry.

Mr. Curr picked up one of the instruments. It was thin and made of metal on three sides. The fourth side had some kind of screw. It was clearly designed to crush sensitive parts of a victim's body.

"Do you know what this is?" Mr. Curr asked. "It's called a C-clamp. No plumber can work without one."

He put it down and picked up a large round device with a handle on one side and a nasty-looking coil of wire coming out of the other. "And this is called a snake. They say it's the plumber's best friend."

Mr. Curr stepped around the desk and waved the snake under my friends' noses. "Now, which one of you is going to talk?"

Woof! I gave them a warning bark. *They couldn't talk, no matter what!* A moment later the choke chain tightened around my neck until I could hardly breathe.

"Want me to get rid of the dog?" Duke asked.

"No!" barked Mr. Curr. "He's important."

"Excuse me, Mr. Curr," said Duke. "How could he be important? He's just a dog."

"Just a dog?" Mr. Curr repeated, gritting his teeth, his eyes bulging with anger. "Let me ask you a question. How many computers did we detect hacking into the city waste treatment system last night?"

"Uh, four, boss," Duke answered.

"And how many computers did we find in that apartment?" Mr. Curr asked.

"Uh, four, boss," Duke said again.

"And how many *people* did we find in the apartment?" Mr. Curr asked.

"Uh, three, boss," answered Duke.

"And what does that tell that microscopic brain of yours?" snarled Mr. Curr.

"Uh, that one of the people was using two computers at once?" Duke guessed.

"No, you idiot!" Mr. Curr shouted. "It means that that dog is one of them!"

"But he's just a dog, boss," said Duke.

"No, he's *not* just a dog," Mr. Curr replied with an icy tone. "He's a highly trained member of the Animal Intelligence Agency and it's because of him that my plot was almost uncovered. And no matter what happens, he is not to leave this office until I say so."

Mr. Curr turned back to my friends and once again waved the snake at them. "I'm losing patience. Which one of you is going to talk?"

Buffhunk talked. I guess I couldn't blame him. That snake was a nasty-looking device.

"Very interesting," Mr. Curr said when Buff was finished. "And you're sure that no one outside your group knows about this?"

Sweat dripped down Buff's face and his lower lip trembled. "No one. We were still looking for the bug when you guys grabbed us this morning."

Mr. Curr pushed a button on the intercom on his desk. "Lance, did you check their e-mail files?"

"Yes, Mr. Curr," a voice replied. "There's no record of any e-mail going out of any of the computers since yesterday."

"Very good." Mr. Curr let go of the intercom button. He turned and faced my friends. "Tough break. You came so close. Too bad no one on the outside knows. So my plan is safe. The deadline is noon today. In a few hours, if my demands are not met, this country will face a nightmare like nothing it has ever faced before!"

110

"Why are you doing this?" Richgurl suddenly asked.

Mr. Curr squinted at her. "Why should I tell you?"

"What does it matter?" Richgurl replied. "There's nothing we can do about it now."

"You want to know why?" Mr. Curr drummed his fingers on his desk thoughtfully. "All right, I'll tell you. I'm doing it because of portable plastic outhouses."

"What?" Foxybabe repeated.

"Look around this office, Granny," Mr. Curr said. "What do you see? What do you think you're sitting in right now?"

"Portable plastic outhouses," Buffhunk said.

"That's right," said Mr. Curr. "You are in the executive offices of Call-A-Can International, the world's biggest manufacturer of portable plastic outhouses. The company was started by my father, O. Bowser Curr."

"So?" said Richgurl.

"A button on my sleeve?" Mr. Curr replied. "Or maybe you'd like to know why the United States is the greatest country on earth? How do you think we were able to build our huge cities, our bridges, tunnels, and highways? With the help of portable plastic outhouses, that's how. Without them, we would be nothing!"

I studied the confused looks on the faces of my friends.

"And let me tell you something else," Mr. Curr

went on. "What do you think happens to a portable plastic outhouse when it gets full? It stops working, that's what! It becomes useless! And do you know what that means?"

"You have to get a new one?" Richgurl guessed.

"Ha!" Mr. Curr chortled insanely. "No, you purple-haired idiot! When a portable plastic outhouse gets full, you have to have someone come and empty it!"

Buffhunk wrinkled his nose. "Yuck!"

Mr. Curr glared at him. His eyes had an evil gleam and his teeth were grinding. "Did you say yuck, fatso?"

Buffhunk nodded meekly.

Mr. Curr narrowed his eyes. "You and all the rest of them." He stood up and stepped over to the window. "Let me tell you something, chubbo. You see this city? You see those highways? That airport? None of that would be here if it wasn't for the man who empties the portable plastic outhouses. None of it! When it comes right down to it, he's the guy who makes it all possible."

"Well, I wouldn't say that," said Foxybabe.

Mr. Curr swung around and stuck his face right in hers. "You wouldn't, Ms. Wrinkle-face? Well, I would. And right now you're handcuffed to a toilet and I'm not."

Mr. Curr glared at the rest of us. "Now I'm going to tell you a story. It's the story of a little boy who was proud of his father. Every morning his

112

father woke up and put on his work clothes and got in his tank truck and went to work. And every night he came home. Maybe we were dog poor. Maybe he didn't smell so good, but he worked hard to put bread on our table and a roof over our heads. I was proud of my father. I thought he was the greatest man alive. . . . Until that terrible day."

"What day?" Richgurl asked.

"The day my first-grade teacher, Ms. Stake, had each of us get up in front of the classroom and tell what our parents did. I went up to the front of the room and I told everyone what my dad did. . . ." Mr. Curr's voice trailed off. Tears came to his eyes and he blinked them back.

"They laughed at you?" Richgurl guessed.

Mr. Curr nodded. He sniffed and wiped the tears out of his eyes. "I tried to stick up for my dad. I tried to explain that without portable plastic outhouses nothing could be built. That if it wasn't for my father, we'd probably all be living in tents and tepees. But they still laughed. Even Ms. Stake laughed. And they gave me a nickname. They called me Crud Boy Curr."

"That's terrible," Richgurl said.

"Yes," agreed Mr. Curr. The evil gleam reappeared in his eyes. "And now I'll have my payback. If they don't give me a billion dollars and the Lincoln Memorial by noon today, I will personally send this country down the drain.

113

Every toilet will stop working. It will be total anarchy."

"And then what?" Foxybabe asked.

"Aha!" Mr. Curr cried. "For once you've asked the right question, you old fleabag! I'll tell you what will happen then. You'll all realize who's really in control. You'll realize that you can't survive without me! And then you'll give me what I want."

"No offense or anything, but what *do* you want a billion dollars for?" asked Buffhunk. "I mean, you've already got this huge company. It looks to me like you must be loaded."

"Of course I am, you tubby blob of protoplasm!" Mr. Curr cried. "I don't need the money. But I want this country to pay. I want them to do what should have been done years ago when I first asked."

"What's that?" asked Richgurl.

"Build a lasting memorial to my father," Mr. Curr said. "And since they never did it, I'm going to use their money to do it."

"Wait a minute!" Richgurl realized. "Why do I think this has something to do with the Lincoln Memorial?"

"Because you're a smart little purple-pierced punkette," Mr. Curr replied. "That's right. I'm going to use the money to rebuild the Lincoln Memorial and name it after my father."

"Why?" asked Foxybabe.

"I'll tell you why, Grandma Miniskirt," Mr.

Curr answered. "Because if you ask most people to name the greatest American who ever lived, they'll probably say Abraham Lincoln. And they'd be *almost* right. Because the truth is, after my father, Abraham Lincoln is probably the *second-greatest* American who ever lived. So in the future when people come here to see the greatest American who ever lived, they'll go to the Lincoln Memorial."

"And find O. Bowser Curr there instead?" guessed Richgurl.

"Exactly!" cried Mr. Curr.

"Okay, I see where this is going," said Buffhunk. "But why should it cost so much? I mean, you'll have to change Lincoln's face and the name on the memorial, but it shouldn't cost a billion dollars."

"That's because you haven't thought it all the way through, you jiggling jar of human Jell-O!" Mr. Curr ranted. "Yes, I'll have to change the face and the name. But that's just the beginning! When you enter the Lincoln Memorial, what do you see?"

"Lincoln sitting in a chair," answered Foxybabe.

"Actually, it's more like a throne," said Buffhunk.

"Precisely!" Mr. Curr cried. "And when I'm finished, it *will* be a throne! The throne every man, woman, and child in this country sits on at least once a day!"

"Oh, noooo!" Foxybabe gasped in horror.

"That's awful!" yelled Buffhunk.

"Actually, it sounds pretty funny," Richgurl chuckled.

"But there's more!" cried Mr. Curr. "After I've finished with Lincoln himself, there's the building around him!"

"But it's a beautiful building," Foxybabe gasped. "Lined with those tall marble columns. Why change it?"

"Because I want to, you dried-up repository of prune juice!" Mr. Curr chortled. "I'm going to tear every one of those columns down and replace the entire structure with a huge, sparkling white —"

"Portable plastic outhouse!" Richgurl cried.

"Precisely," Mr. Curr said with a mad gleam in his eye. "Just think of it. For the rest of time, people will come to our capital to visit the greatest man who ever lived: O. Bowser Curr in his giant portable plastic outhouse."

"You're completely insane," said Foxybabe.

"Thank you," Mr. Curr said in a suddenly calm voice. "All the great men in history were considered insane at one time or another. So all you have done is confirm what I've always known. That I am among the great!"

A moment of silence passed.

"Now what?" Foxybabe asked.

Mr. Curr looked at his watch. "Now . . . we wait."

Mr. Curr checked his watch, then shook his head.

"How disappointing," he said. "It's ten past noon. The deadline has been passed and my demands have been ignored. Just as I expected, they still won't take me seriously. Well, they're about to find out that I'm a man of my word. Twelve hours from now, every toilet in this country will back up and stop working."

Mr. Curr turned to his computer and began to type.

"Wait!" Buffhunk said. "What if they're trying to meet your demands and it's just taking longer than they thought it would? What if two or three hours from now they agree to what you want? Will it be too late?"

Mr. Curr stopped typing and looked up. "No. I can stop it all. Even a few seconds before midnight. But it won't happen, chubski. You and I both know the government has never taken me seriously. But they will after tonight."

He started typing again. I knew he must have been activating sewer bugs in all of our country's major sewage treatment plants. Buffhunk, Foxybabe, Richgurl, and I exchanged nervous looks.

"What about us?" Foxybabe asked.

Mr. Curr looked up from his computer. "What about you?"

"Can't you let us go?" asked Buffhunk. "I mean, there's no reason to keep us. It's too late for anyone to stop you now."

"Do you think I'm that stupid?" Mr. Curr growled. "Of course I won't let you go. There are hundreds of ways you could still stop me. My whole plan is based on the element of surprise. You're not going anywhere. You're staying right here until it's time to move to my secret bunker."

"Secret bunker?" Richgurl repeated.

"Yes," said Mr. Curr. "With its own private water supply and sewer system."

"Of course!" said Buffhunk. "So that you won't have to suffer with everyone else."

"Why should I?" asked Mr. Curr. "I've suffered my whole life. The indignities of being made fun of because of my father. Being called Crud Boy Curr. Revenge will be sweet."

"And sort of smelly," added Richgurl.

Time was running out. Mr. Curr had worked steadily at his computer for hours. I didn't doubt for a second that he was hacking into sewage treatment plants all over the country and activating the bugs that would clog up toilets everywhere.

Outside it had grown dark. Buffhunk, Foxybabe, and Richgurl were still handcuffed to their portable plastic outhouses. I was still wearing the choke chain. Innocent people everywhere were getting ready to celebrate the beginning of the new year, the new decade, the new century, the new millennium. They were looking forward to a truly historic moment.

It would be historic, all right. But not in a way any of them could possibly imagine.

Finally, at ten minutes before midnight, Mr. Curr turned off his computer. He pressed a button on the intercom on his desk. "Lance and

Duke, it's time. I'll finish up at one second before midnight."

The door opened and the two burly thugs came in.

"Take them downstairs," Mr. Curr ordered.

Lance took Buffhunk and Foxybabe. Duke took Richgurl and me. They led us out of the office and down in the elevator to the lobby. The street outside was filled with gaily dressed party-goers on their way to celebrate the new millennium. Hardly any of them noticed the dark van parked at the curb. The other two thugs from the apartment break-in waited beside it.

We stopped just inside the lobby doors.

"We can't take you out there in handcuffs," Mr. Curr said. "Someone might notice. So Duke's going to take the handcuffs off you one at a time and take you out to the van and hand you over to Sparky and Chief. Lance is going to stay here in the lobby with the others. I advise you not to try anything funny."

One by one, Duke took Buffhunk, Foxybabe, and Richgurl out to the van. Finally, I was alone in the lobby with Mr. Curr and Lance.

"All right, pup, it's your turn." Mr. Curr gave my leash a yank. The choke chain tightened painfully around my neck. "No funny stuff and no barking or I'll pull that chain so tight you'll spend the rest of your life sounding like a Chihuahua with laryngitis."

I stared through the glass doors and across the sidewalk to the van parked at the curb. This was it. The end of my mission. Once I got into that van, it was all over. I'd be taken with the others to that secret bunker and kept there until it was too late. I'd failed. I'd let my country down. The AIA was right. I was a has-been, an old washed-up dog who deserved to be retired.

I hung my head. Mr. Curr yanked on the leash and I started to follow. Lance held the door open for us.

We stepped out onto the sidewalk. The air was cool and dark. After hours in that fragrance-filled office, I welcomed the fresh scent of car exhaust, asphalt, and human B.O. From far in the distance came the sounds of music, laughter, and fireworks as people began to celebrate.

Little did they know that they were about to face the worst calamity of their lives.

Across the sidewalk, Duke pushed open the van's doors. Inside I saw Buffhunk, Foxybabe, and Richgurl guarded by the thugs Sparky and Chief. My friends had grim, sad faces. Like me, they knew they'd failed.

Mr. Curr tugged on the leash and I headed toward the van.

And then, out of nowhere, someone shouted, "Byte!"

Everyone turned. Way down at the end of the block a boy was running toward us.

"Byte!" he cried again. It was Benjy Barkley!

"Hurry!" Mr. Curr yelled at Lance.

Lance dashed around to the driver's side of the van. Mr. Curr yanked hard on my collar to get me inside.

"Byte! Wait!" Benjy screamed as he ran toward us. *"Stop! Leave him alone!"*

People on the sidewalk were turning their heads. Benjy was running as hard as he could. I couldn't imagine what he was doing on the streets of the capital at almost midnight on New Year's Eve.

"Mom, Dad, Brandy!" Benjy shouted back over his shoulder as he ran. *"I found him. Hurry! They're trying to steal him!"*

Now the rest of the Barkleys came running around the corner!

"Hey!" Mr. Barkley yelled. *"Let go of that dog! What do you think you're doing?"*

"Leave him alone!" Brandy shouted as she ran. *"He's our dog!"*

Mr. Curr stared in amazement as the Barkleys ran toward him. Suddenly I saw my chance. I quickly made a circle around him, wrapping the leash around his legs.

"What the — ?" Mr. Curr looked down, but it was too late. I gave the leash a good solid yank.

"Yikes!" Mr. Curr's feet went out from under him and he crashed to the sidewalk. His cell phone tumbled out of his jacket and clattered against the concrete.

The Barkleys were getting closer. They were only a dozen yards away when, *bang*, a sound like a pistol shot rang out.

I crouched down on the sidewalk. For a second I thought someone had been shot. The Barkleys dove for the ground all around me.

But it was only a firecracker. Duke grabbed the van door and tried to close it, but just at that moment, Buffhunk stuck his leg out.

"Ow!" Buffhunk cried as the door slammed into his leg and bounced back open.

"Pee Soop!" came a shout from inside the van.

A split second later, the thug named Chief sailed out of the van and crashed facefirst to the sidewalk. Duke tried to close the door again just as Buffhunk tried to get out.

"Ow!" Buffhunk cried as the door slammed into his shoulder and bounced open. "Stop doing that!"

"Arghhh!" Sparky tumbled out of the van with Richgurl's studded black dog collar strapped tightly around his neck.

"Get up, you idiots!" Mr. Curr yelled as he

124

struggled to his feet. Once again I yanked on the leash and brought him down.

Meanwhile, the Barkleys were getting up. Buffhunk staggered out of the van, followed by Richgurl and Foxybabe.

"Cheep-tea!" Foxybabe screamed as she karate-chopped Lance on the back of the neck and sent him flying headfirst into the side of the van.

A total melee broke out. It looked like a real dogfight. Richgurl jumped on Sparky's back and choked him with her dog collar. Buffhunk body-slammed Duke, then sat on him. Foxybabe head-butted Chief into Sparky.

In the middle of the fracas, I snuck over to Mr. Curr's cell phone lying on the sidewalk. There was something I had to do, and I had to do it fast.

I turned my back to the Barkleys so they wouldn't be able to see as I quickly keyed a phone number into the cell phone.

A second later I looked up. Mr. Curr's thugs were sprawled on the sidewalk. Buffhunk, Rich-gurl, and Foxybabe stood over them. *What a team!*

"Byte!" I felt a pair of eight-year-old arms slide around my neck and hug me. "Oh, Byte, are you okay? I'm so happy to see you!"

"Hold it right there, Mr. Dognapper," I heard Mr. Barkley say to Mr. Curr. "You're not going anywhere!"

"But you don't understand," Mr. Curr lied. "I've never seen this dog before in my life. I was just walking along and I found him."

Ruff! Ruff! Grrrrrr! I barked loudly, snarled, and shook my head.

"Byte doesn't seem to agree," said Brandy.

"I think you better stay right where you are," said Mr. Barkley. He turned to Mrs. Barkley. "Get out your cell phone, hon. Call the police."

Screeech! No sooner had Mrs. Barkley finished calling than two black cars skidded around the corner and screeched to a stop.

"Wow, that was fast!" Benjy said.

Only I knew it wasn't the police. The door of one car swung open and Lassie jumped out, followed by a man and a woman wearing blue windbreakers with AIA in big yellow letters on the back. Lassie pointed at Mr. Curr.

"Is this the person we've been looking for, Byte?" she asked.

Arf! I nodded.

"Good work," Lassie said. She turned to the man and woman in the windbreakers. "Take him away."

The man and woman pulled Mr. Curr to his feet and dragged him into the back of the car. Meanwhile, AIA agents from the second car grabbed Mr. Curr's thugs. Lassie stepped over and gave my head a rub. "I'm proud of you, Byte."

Then she turned to leave.

Woof! I barked. Wasn't she forgetting something?

"Oh, of course. Sorry, I was just distracted." Lassie reached into her pocket and tossed me a dog biscuit. Then she got into the front of the black car.

"What was that all about?" Mr. Barkley asked as both cars sped away into the night.

"That red-haired lady looked vaguely familiar," said Mrs. Barkley.

"Ask Byte," said Brandy. "She talked to him like she knew him."

The Barkleys all looked down at me with curious expressions. I sat up with my mouth open and my tongue hanging out, panting happily and wagging my tail.

"Wait a minute!" Mr. Barkley said. "What are we waiting for Byte to do? He can't talk. He's just a dog."

Suddenly we heard loud explosions all around us. The sky above us grew bright with bursts of light as people everywhere launched fireworks. The air was filled with honking car horns and tooting sirens and cheers.

"Happy new year, everyone!" Mr. Barkley shouted. The Barkleys hugged one another.

Benjy put his arms around my neck and squeezed. "Happy new year, Byte! It wouldn't have been the same without you."

A few mornings later I was lying in bed, thinking about the Barkleys. I guess I was wrong about them. They really did care. Why else would they spend the biggest New Year's Eve of their lives wandering around the capital, looking for me?

A little while later they came into the kitchen for breakfast. Once again, Mr. Barkley was carrying a phone bill. He had a puzzled look on his face.

"Uh-oh," Brandy said. "Don't tell me the phantom phoner has been at it again."

Mr. Barkley nodded. "Yup. But you want to hear something *really* strange? There was a whole bunch of nights just before New Year's Eve when no one used the phone."

"What's so strange about that?" Mrs. Barkley asked.

"They were the exact same nights that Byte was gone," Mr. Barkley said.

The next thing I knew, the whole Barkley family was staring at me. I sat up, let my tongue hang out, and started to pant.

"You think it's possible?" Mrs. Barkley asked.

"I don't know what to think," replied Mr. Barkley. "I mean, we all know that Byte was up to something. We just never found out what."

That much was true. Despite how close the country had come to complete disaster, not a word about it had ever appeared in a newspaper or on TV. The AIA had managed to keep the whole thing secret. The world would never know how close it came to Total Toilet Backup.

The Barkleys were still staring at me. I decided to roll over on my back and invite them to give me a good belly scratch. Maybe that would distract them.

"Oh, I don't know," said Brandy as she kneeled down and started to scratch my tummy. "I think maybe we're just imagining things. I mean, look at this cute dog. All he wants is to be loved."

WEDNESDAY, JANUARY 5, 2000
1030 HRS

Later that day I was lying on the kitchen floor, enjoying a snooze in the midwinter sun, when I heard a scratching sound coming from outside. I opened one eye.

It was the calico cat! With a jerk of her head, she gave me the sign that I was to come outside and follow her.

I heaved myself up and went out. The calico cat led me out of the yard and down the street. A school bus was parked at the corner. That was strange. The kids had gone to school hours ago.

Through the windshield I saw the bus driver. She nodded and I caught a flash of red. Now I understood. I trotted over to the door. Lassie opened it.

"Hop in, Byte," she said.

I climbed up. Lassie closed the bus door behind me. I cocked my head and gave her a curious look.

"Good news, my friend," she said. "The AIA was so impressed with your work that they've decided to make an exception and let you return to active duty. Your retirement's over. You can come back."

It was the last thing I expected and I admit it took me by surprise. I didn't know what to bark.

Lassie frowned. "I thought you'd jump for joy, Byte."

So did I. And yet, all I could think about was the Barkleys. Leave them again? And this time maybe for good?

Ruff. I shook my head.

Lassie blinked and her eyes went wide. "You're saying no?"

I nodded.

"Are you sure?" Lassie asked.

Arf.

Lassie pursed her lips. She reached down and rubbed my head. "Okay, Byte, I'll be sorry not to have you, but I know you must have a good reason."

Lassie opened the bus door again. "Have a good life, pup."

I went down the steps, but before I got off the bus, I looked back over my shoulder at her. I felt a tug at my heart.

Woof! Here's barking at you, kid.

WEDNESDAY, JANUARY 5, 2000
2345 HRS

That night I visited the private chat room. My friends were already there.

Buffhunk: Hey, Byte, where u been? We've been w8ing 4 u.

Byte: Had to lie low. My family's beginning 2 suspect something. I h8 2 say it, but this will be my last time.

Richgurl: Oh, Byte, are u sure?

Byte: Afraid so.

Foxybabe: We'll miss u.

Byte: I'll miss u guys, 2.

Buffhunk: Listen, Byte, before u go, I just want 2 thank u for bringing us into the mission. Because of what we did, the CIA is giving me my old job back.

Foxybabe: I have good news, 2. As a reward 4 our mission, the NSA has increased my pension. I'm moving 2 an old age home in Hawaii!

Byte: That's gr8, guys. I'm really happy for u.

Richgurl: Here's my good news. The FBI's going 2 give me a full scholarship to the college of my choice.

Byte: Fantastic!

Buffhunk: What about u, Byte? They must've done something nice 4 u 2.

Byte: They offered me a position with the AIA.

Richgurl: That's gr8! Congrats!

Buffhunk: Way 2 go, Byte!

Byte: Thanks, guys, but I told them no.

Foxybabe: What? Why?

Byte: Our mission taught me a lesson. It may be really exciting 2 be a secret agent. But nothing beats being a dog in a family that loves u.

Richgurl: Aw, Byte, that's really sweet.

Foxybabe: U're a good dog.

Buffhunk: We'll miss u, Byte.

Byte: Stay well, my friends, and be good.

That is the story of how my chat room friends and I saved the country for Y2K. I won't blame you if you find it hard to understand why I chose not to have the exciting life of a secret agent. And why I'm happier just hanging around the house, sleeping in the sun and getting scratched where it itches.

But believe me. I made the right choice. Life is good when you know you're loved.

Over the past few months I've gotten used to retirement. Now that the weather is getting warm, I think I may even take up golf. Mr. Barkley belongs to a local club. Eighteen holes seems like a lot, but I'm hoping he'll agree to play nine with a canine.

Finally, there's one last thing. Sometimes Benjy or Brandy takes me for a walk and we pass a construction site where a new house or building is going up. Usually there'll be a portable plastic outhouse nearby.

I'll never look at one of those things the same way again.

About the Author

Todd Strasser has written many award-winning novels for young and teenage readers. Among his best-known books are *Help! I'm Trapped in Obedience School* and *Help! I'm Trapped in Santa's Body*. His most recent books for Scholastic are *Help! I'm Trapped in a Movie Star's Body* and *Help! I'm Trapped in My Lunch Lady's Body*.

The movie *Next to You*, starring Melissa Joan Hart, was based on his novel *How I Created My Perfect Prom Date*.

Todd speaks frequently at schools about the craft of writing and conducts writing workshops for young people. He and his family live outside New York City with their yellow Labrador retriever, Mac.

You can find out more about Todd and his books at http://www.toddstrasser.com